Good News…?

Good News...?

an anthology

Edited by Debz Hobbs-Wyatt and Gill James

Bridge House

British Library Cataloguing in Publication Data

A Record of this Publication is available from the British
Library

ISBN 978-1-914199-88-2

This edition published 2024 by Bridge House Publishing
Manchester, England

Contents

5

Introduction

We set quite a challenge this time. We asked for Good News stories. We all know good news doesn't sell newspapers. Bad news at least bring challenges to the protagonists. What if good news just means that everything is going our characters' way? Where will we find story then?

Good news often means change. It can also rob you of the opportunity of being a victim.

Then sometimes something might look like good news. It may be exactly what you wished for but it may not be what you need. You need to be careful about what you wish for.

It was as ever difficult to make our choices. Both judges looked at every single story without knowing the identity of the writer. We awarded points for how much story there was, how well the writer had addressed the theme, what the writing was like and how professional the writer had been. We overlapped a lot in our choices with us both having fourteen stories in the top twenty. The remaining ten were in both of our top thirties.

It is exciting when we have finished our deliberations and we reveal the names. It's a little disappointing if we find we've rejected some writers we've published before. On the other hand, it's great to recognise old friends and welcome new writers into our community.

We hope you enjoy this collection. You can read more short stories on our CaféLit site
https://www.cafelitmagazine.uk
and you can find a lot of books similar to this one in our online shop:
https://www.thebridgetowncafebooksshop.co.uk.

Happy reading

Anna's Secret Mission

Sara Knapp

Yes, Constable Dale, I've seen the footage. And yes, I certainly can understand why the detective alerted you. Definitely on the ball, there.
But there's a perfectly good justification for what you've seen. It just might take time to explain. All the time in the world? Right. I'll try my best...
Every family has its stories. Funny, tragic, weird.

For example, my grandma's neighbours, the Dobbs, met twenty-odd years ago when they got stuck in one of those see-through lifts in a shopping-centre. He has no head for heights. She's claustrophobic. But they were practically engaged by the time they were rescued.

And my best mate Emma and her siblings were all born, several years apart, in the first week of August. People speculate on how their parents celebrate Bonfire Night.

What? Yes, I do think it's relevant, Constable. I'm scene-setting.

My family anecdotes, though, tend not to have happy endings. For example, way back, my dad's dad had a £50,000 win on something called The Football Pools. The cheque came as a total surprise. My grandma was at the bus-stop across the road, so he rushed over to tell her, and was killed by a Number 9.

And when my aunty Jo won a crystal decanter at a fete, she tripped on the way out, crashing to the ground and landing on her prize. She bled loads and the scar is *huge*.

So we never place bets, do the lottery or buy scratch cards. We don't Guess The Weight Of The Cake. If someone runs a raffle, we may donate, but we refuse the ticket. It's safer that way.

Yes, Constable. Idiosyncratic maybe, but then you haven't seen my aunty's scar. Where was I?

So: I often shop for my gran, and sometimes her friend Sue who, ever since a phantom pineapple mysteriously added itself to our bill, likes to "check receipts properly". If I'd been paying attention, maybe I'd have noticed the coupon attached to my receipt. But evidently I wasn't. The woman in front of me at the check-out, though, turning to make sure she'd packed everything, squealed: "Oooh look, you've got a 'Pop-Me-In!' coupon," plucked it from my hand, and "popped it in" to a cardboard pretend computer thingy by the door. Which shook and pushed out (I think it's faulty) *several* red tickets.

"There you go, dear – that'll be nice, won't it?" she said, puzzlingly, dropping them into my carrier, and headed off. The person queueing behind me coughed meaningfully, so I took my shopping and left.

I forgot all about the tickets until I was sorting stuff (me, Gran, Sue) on my kitchen table. I gave a squawk when found them. They were supermarket vouchers worth £15, £25 and £50.

Now you can see the problem, can't you, Constable? Can't you? Well...

These vouchers were of course, indisputably, "winnings". And as established earlier, my family doesn't "do" winnings. They bring Bad Things.

I groaned, grabbed Gran's and Sue's bags and headed off. Clutching the three blood-red rectangular omens...

What? Yes, Constable Dale. I am getting to the point. Actually, I just had an idea. I happen to know that Sue would absolutely love to meet a real policeman! Maybe you'd like to interview her? You'll see? OK. Where was I?

Well, quite logically, my grandma and I – given the family history, which I have been at pains to explain – felt that there should be no tempting fate. We couldn't use the vouchers for Personal Gain.

And Sue decided that, out of loyalty, she would align herself with us – after all, Gran's her best friend – and that therefore, she too would decline to use any of the vouchers. This left us with the problem of what to do with the blessed things. But the answer to that came to us all simultaneously, I think. The vouchers should go to "deserving shoppers", as defined by yours truly, Anna Blake. Designated Shopper.

Aha. I think you are on my wavelength now, Constable Dale? No?

So I was charged – ha, ha – on my next trip, conveniently close to Christmas, with what I and my, um, *accomplices* have christened "Shop-Gifting". I limbered up by slipping the £15 voucher into the bag of an old lady who'd only bought yellow sticker stuff. I did that near the bus-stop; maybe the CCTV doesn't pick things up beyond the car-park? Anyway, the cashiers will know if the woman with the purple coat and the white hat with those ear-flap things has used a voucher. Or maybe just looked a bit happier of recent…

I think I can tell what you are going to say, but I'll just finish, if I may.

Now, your CCTV footage there shows Mission 2: the £25 "drop", so to speak. The voucher is squeezed between my fingers as I flip it into the man's carrier. I expect it is zoom-in-on-able? I did have to drop my brolly so he'd bend down to retrieve it. That's a technique Gran and Sue hit upon; I must say it worked a treat. Good job they're on the right side of the law.

Pardon? Yes, I realise you'll have to check this out. But since it's perfectly verifiable, I have no worries. Well, save the obvious one…

What? Well, the blindingly obvious fact that I have not yet carried out The Biggie! The £50 voucher "drop".

Actually, it occurs to me, Constable Dale, that were you able to accompany me on my final mission, you would constitute the perfect distraction. If you were to engage the young mum I've nominated (two little girls, she has, and such a tired smile) in conversation, I'm sure I could Do The Deed and slide that £50 voucher in her bag easy as pie!

You would?!

A condition? What condition?

Oh. Well. Now you mention it, a glass of something to celebrate a final act of shop-gifting would not seem inappropriate. OK – it's a date!

Good news! Our family luck may just be changing...

About the author

Sara Knapp was born in Manchester (UK). A sometime translator and teacher, she has always loved reading and listening to stories of all genres. She has published non-fiction, short stories in *Yours Fiction* and more recently in sci-fi anthology *AI, Robot* (JayHenge Publishing KB).

Cinderella Rising

Penny Rogers

Alan died early on a cold morning in January. Since Aunt June had passed away we'd become closer; he was cantankerous right to the end, but I'd grown quite fond of him. I opened the back door in spite of the bitter cold, glad of the fresh air. Snow lay thick across the garden, drifting against the east side of the house. The driving wind blew spiky flakes against my face and into the kitchen.

In his bed the old man looked peaceful. It seemed a shame to move him, so I decided to wait until daylight before calling the doctor. I made another cup of tea and considered Fiona and Dion. They would be in Mexico by now.

I thought back to my arrival, just two days earlier. My reception that Friday evening was every bit as frosty as the conditions outside.

"And what time do you call this?" Fiona muttered, terse as usual.

"Give me a break, Fiona, it was a dreadful drive; snow, ice, fog, vehicles all over the place. Any chance of a cuppa?"

"Help yourself." My cousin wasn't even going to make it for me. I put the kettle on.

"How's Alan?" I hoped that talking about her dad might improve Fiona's mood.

"He's old, sick and difficult. Why are you so late?"

"I told you, the weather is awful. Just look outside if you don't believe me."

"You should've left more time."

"Fiona, be reasonable. I can't just walk out of work. I leave as soon as I can but I can't just push off."

"Anyway, I've got some good news," she announced.

"Dion and I are getting married next week." I knew that she and the local celebrity photographer were an item, but had no idea this was on the cards. Now I found out that the wedding was to be in Cancun, followed by an extended honeymoon exploring South America.

"What about Alan?" I asked.

"He's your problem now. He took you in when you had no one. The least you can do is look after him now. I'm going to bed. I've got a long journey tomorrow." Fiona disappeared into her bedroom for the last time. The kettle was boiling. I made my tea, going through the routine like an automaton.

The next day I emailed my boss requesting emergency leave. I hoped he'd be sympathetic, we were short-staffed as usual, but for the moment I had other things to worry about. Fiona packed, said goodbye to her dad and left in a taxi that afternoon.

Alan looked so frail. She'd told him she was going on holiday, no mention of the wedding or extended honeymoon, but I think he knew something was up.

And that was it really. By late afternoon on Sunday Alan's breathing was very bad and the last vestige of colour had drained from his pallid face. The room was warm, but his skin felt cold and clammy. I tried to get him to drink, but he didn't want anything. So I just sat by him and waited.

I was glad I'd sorted things out before Alan got too ill. Fiona must have known he was deteriorating but she probably thought she'd run off with her photographer, get married and come back from her honeymoon when she got the news that her dad had died. The thought of Fiona and Dion together gave me the determination to see my scheme through. Over the years my boyfriends had all been scared off by Alan and June, and later Fiona. Everyone I brought home had been subjected to searching questions about income and prospects, as well as innuendo about my former relationships. When I met Joe I really tried to keep him away from them to give us a chance. I think Fiona wanted me to stay single so that I could be called upon to help out at a moment's notice. Whatever her motive, as soon as Fiona knew there was a special man in my life she caused all sorts of difficulties; calling me at odd hours about trivial matters, coming to my flat and causing a scene, even putting unflattering photos and unkind remarks about me on social media. He got fed up and left.

My unwitting allies in my plan to get even had been the Colliers who lived at the end of the road. At some point Fiona had upset them; I never got to the bottom of what had gone on, something to do with what their terrier had done, or not done. Whatever had happened, they had no time for each other and hadn't spoken for ages. This elderly couple were the perfect solution to my problem.

It was early December when the chance came. I had been writing cards and wrapping presents. Alan was still quite well and enjoying the extra indulgence he got over Christmas.

"Uncle Alan," I asked, "would you like to write a Christmas card for Fiona?"

"Could do. You write it for me." He didn't sound very enthusiastic.

"Well, it would mean a lot to her if you wrote it. Look, I've got this one with snowdrops on it."

"Didn't think she liked flowers. Give it here."

I got out the card and a sheet of paper.

"Have a go anyway. Try your name first on this piece of paper. Tell you what. Write your name on it, I'll do the love to Fiona bit, then I'll get you a glass of sherry."

And it worked. To be honest I felt uncomfortable about tricking him. Then I remembered all the times that he and June had been mean to me, so I just got on with what I had to do. The card with snowdrops and a sugary greeting to his daughter was there, on top of the sheet of paper. I went to help his shaky hand.

"I can do it" he grumbled. "Where's that sherry?" Fortunately his poor eyesight prevented him from seeing the paper underneath the card. "Why don't you write your full name?" I conspicuously clinked the sherry bottle against the glass. "Large one?"

So he did it. Alan Jeffrey Williams signed his name in a clear, if spidery, hand right across the bottom of the piece of paper, not the card.

All I had to do was write "Love, Dad" on the snowdrop card. And put everything else in a safe place.

After Alan had drunk his sherry he dropped off to sleep. I guessed I had about an hour before he woke up, so quickly retrieving my bag of papers I went down to see the Colliers. I took them a Christmas card and a box of biscuits. They invited me in and got out the port. I explained that I needed them to witness Alan's will. We all agreed it was too icy to bring Alan to them and there was no need to drag them out into the cold either; after all they'd known each other for many years. The Colliers witnessed Alan's signature and then asked if I could help them with their wills. They found the terminology difficult and failing eyesight didn't help either of them. It was no trouble to ensure the wording on their wills was unambiguous and I was soon on my way home, Alan's will safely in my bag.

Often there are snowdrops in the garden in January, poking their luminous heads through the cold ground to herald the still distant spring. This year it had been so cold, and such a lot of snow and ice they hadn't had a chance. But it was still early and I knew they were there, safe under their chilly blanket waiting for the right moment. My plan was ready, I had to be like the snowdrops and wait until everything was right before I put it into action. It had been easy to use the internet to get what I needed. I had done it months ago and it was all ready. All I had to do was bide my time.

Fiona didn't like her dad's house; it was too big and old-fashioned for her. I loved it, especially the garden.

I thought about all the times that my cousin had been given things that were denied to me. I must have been about ten when I asked, "Why can't I learn ballet?" as Fiona was being taken to her dancing class one Saturday morning. Aunt June's reply was "because your feet are too big."

Another time I asked, "Fiona's got riding lessons for her birthday, why can't I?" Uncle Alan answered, "You're older and need to spend more time on your homework. And help your aunt in the house." Fiona never helped, not even to dry the dishes. I was a real life Cinderella.

Things came to a head for me when Fiona got a car for her twenty-first birthday. I was furious. When I was twenty-one I had been given a necklace that had belonged to my mum; I reckoned that it was mine anyway. But they made a big thing about giving it to me.

Of course I was glad to have my mum's necklace, I wear it most days, and on the whole I was grateful to Alan and June. They had given me a home, and whatever was left over from their own daughter. Far better than a children's home or living with strangers, but I was always second-best. Alan told me that there was nothing for me in his will, he'd done all he could for me and Fiona would inherit everything. I suppose that's when the seeds of revenge were sown.

At about 6.00 on that Monday morning the snow stopped and I walked into the garden, my footsteps breaking the smooth beauty of the snow. In the darkness a robin sang. It must have sensed the dawn slowly coming from the east: a new day. Fiona and Dion were probably just going to bed in Cancun. I should text her to tell her that Alan was dead. I didn't.

At 9.00 I called the surgery. Dr Jones came very quickly given the treacherous roads, and certified that one of her oldest patients had passed away. She was concerned about me being there on my own with him at the end and more than a little scathing about the absence of his only daughter. I assured her that I was OK, that Fiona deserved her chance of happiness and that it was my duty as a grateful niece to be there as needed. I was so plausible! I almost believed myself.

After the doctor and the undertakers had gone I had the house to myself. I looked round the familiar rooms; soon they would be mine.

I scattered Alan's ashes among the drifts of snowdrops that appeared as the snow melted. I let Alan's solicitor break the sad news of her dad's passing to the newly-wed Fiona.

A week later I heard from the solicitor that Fiona and Dion were on their way to Mexico City when the bus they were travelling in overturned and plunged into a river killing all on board. I pretended to be devastated to learn this, but it really was a stroke of luck as there was now no one to challenge Alan's new will, witnessed by the Colliers, that I found down the back of his favourite chair.

The following autumn Mrs Collier died. After the funeral I hosted a wake for friends and neighbours as they had no family. Mr Collier didn't live very long on his own after losing his wife, and now their lovely house is also mine thanks to their explicit generosity to me in their wills. I'm keeping an eye on number 42. It looks as if an elderly lady is moving in. She might need some help.

About the author

Penny Rogers lives in Dorset. She writes mostly short stories, flash fiction and poems and facilitates an informal writing group. She has been published in *CaféLit*, *Funny Pearls*, *Friday Flash Fiction*, *Bare Fiction*, *Potato Soup Journal*, *Paragraph Planet* and in anthologies from Bridge House Publishing, Dorset Writers Network and Henshaw Press. Penny has been shortlisted for the Bridport Prize for Flash Fiction, runner up in the Mani Literary Festival Competition and longlisted for the Plaza Prose Poetry Prize. When she's not writing Penny makes jams, pickles and preserves and knits socks.

18

Doc's Last Trip

Ian Inglis

"I don't believe it," said Alison, when Tim told her the news. "£32,000! He's more than fifty years old."

"That's why," her brother explained. "Take a look on the websites. There's a huge demand for classic vehicles in good condition – you'd be amazed how much people will pay. And Doc is in superb condition. It solves the problem of what to do with him; the buyer's delighted – he can't wait to get his hands on him, although I've explained he'll have to wait for a month or so; and the money will pay the initial fees for Dad's care home. It's good news all round!"

"It's not my idea of good news," interrupted Marcie. "Who's going to tell Dad? Not me."

"Maybe he won't notice."

"He'll notice. He goes in the garage to look at him every day. Sits in him sometimes, for hours on end."

"So long as he doesn't try to drive him."

"Don't worry," said Tim. "I've hidden the keys."

"Dad's not the only one who'll be upset. I know we have to sell him – we agreed on that – but I'm going to be sorry to see him go," Alison said. "I really loved those holidays."

They all did. Once a year, toward the end of April, Tim and his two sisters, Alison and Marcie, would arrive home from school to find the garage doors open wide, a collection of bags, cases, tools, buckets, sponges and boxes scattered around the drive, and pools of soapy water trickling down over the pavement. In the midst of it all sat Doc, his blue-and-white paintwork, polished chrome, and leather interior gleaming proudly.

19

"Well," their father would say, "what do you think? How's he looking? Good for another year?"

While Marcie and Alison – excited as they were – would feign a degree of indifference, Tim's joy was unrestrained. Doc's annual appearance heralded the possibility of unlimited adventures, strange places, the seaside, the countryside, the chance to meet old friends, opportunities to make new friends. Day trips, long weekends, summer holidays, on the Yorkshire coast, in the mountains of Snowdonia and the resorts of North Wales, taking the long road to Devon and Cornwall, or to Edinburgh and the Highlands, the Peak District, the Lake District, the Dales, even occasional journeys on the Cross-Channel Ferry from Dover to Calais, before heading west toward the coastal towns of Brittany and Normandy. Blue skies, sunshine, picnics, barbecues…

The reality of course was rather different. Just as common were the traffic jams, queues, muddy camping and caravan sites, primitive toilet blocks, breakdowns, urgent calls to the AA, unexpected delays, rain thrumming on Doc's roof for hours at a time. And yet, at the end of each trip, there was always a sense of satisfaction, of something gained, a shared understanding that the family bond had somehow been tightened, renewed, strengthened.

"He didn't let us down, did he?" their father would ask. "Got us there and back in one piece. Shall we do it again?"

And they did. Year after year. How could they not? Doc was part of the family. A 1969 Volkswagen Type 2 Dormobile Camper Van, with a 1600 cc engine, a candy-stripe canopy, front-mounted spare wheel, and rear aluminium roof-rack. Bought second-hand, at a bargain price, from a family emigrating to Australia. Low mileage. Registration number DOC 198G.

Eventually, of course, the children ceased to be children:

they left home, holidayed with their friends, went to university, trained for various professions, found work, took jobs in other cities, married, had their own children, divorced, re-married. But Doc remained. Safely closeted in the garage, protected by a large canvas tarpaulin, brought out once or twice a year for a brief outing or an appearance at one of the annual rallies to which Volkswagen enthusiasts would travel in stately procession from all parts of the country. Lovingly maintained, rust-free, spotless. Still immaculate.

But now, there were important decisions to be made. Soon after their mother's death, it became apparent to Tim, Alison and Marcie that their father – now in his mid-eighties – would very soon be unable to continue living by himself. He was becoming forgetful, unpredictable, quick to anger, confused, frustrated; a fall on the stairs, a couple of minor accidents in the kitchen. Options were discussed: carers, a nursing home, sheltered accommodation. He was not excluded from these discussions, but played no active part in them. When they, his three children, met at his house to determine his future, he sat passively in the same room, in front of the television, looking up at them from time to time, wondering why they were there, vaguely reacting to the odd word or phrase. As he dozed and they debated, a tentative plan began to take shape. There'd still be a lot to do. There were their mother's clothes, untouched, upstairs – somebody would have to sort them out. And her collection of dolls. His books, hundreds of them – who would want them? What about the furniture? Things would have to be sold. The house, of course. And then there was Doc.

Their father opened his eyes, pushed himself up from the armchair, and walked slowly over to where they were sitting around the dining table. He stared at Tim menacingly.

"You're a mean bastard, Philip Warren," he said. "Why can't you leave Penny alone?"

"Not again," sighed Alison.

"What's this?" asked Marcie, mystified.

"Dad's developed an obsession with that awful soap on Channel 4. He thinks Tim is one of the characters called Philip Warren, A local thug who attacked the vicar's wife."

"Awkward. What do you do, Tim?"

"What can I do? Play along with him." He turned to face his father. "I know, Mr Fletcher. I'm sorry. I've learned my lesson."

"I'm glad to hear it, son. Because if you ever do anything like that again, you'll have me to deal with."

He sat down, temporarily appeased.

"Well, that rather proves my point," whispered Marcie. "If the mere sight of Tim does that to him, imagine what'll happen when he sees someone driving away with Doc!"

They sat quietly, watching the old man as he fell asleep again, snoring faintly. He who had never seemed to need sleep at all, he who was always the last to go to bed and the first to rise. Alison reached across and squeezed Tim's hand.

"It's so bloody unfair. He's gone downhill so quickly since Mum died—"

"Often happens," Marcie said.

"I know, I know. He loved Doc – we all did – so much. Saying goodbye to him will break his heart. I suppose he's the last link with the past. You know, when we were kids, all the days out, the journeys we made, the family holidays, how excited we all were. I think they were probably the happiest times of Dad's life. Now look at him," she murmured sadly. "Look at all of us. If only we could…"

The gap in the conversation grew longer. The dull drone from the television seemed to diminish. Each of them remained perfectly still, as if any movement would endanger whatever thoughts and memories they were nurturing. Tim stared straight ahead, conscious that his sisters were watching him, waiting for him to speak.

"I can," said Tim. "Alison?"

She nodded.

"Yes."

"Marcie?"

"I can't. No."

"Marcie," they said.

"Oh, alright. If we must. Yes."

"Where are we going?"

"Bakewell, Dad. You know, in Derbyshire?"

"Never heard of it."

"You'll remember it when we get there."

Tim was driving, his father next to him in the passenger seat. Alison and Marcie were sharing the rear couch. In the three weeks since they'd reached their decision, they'd explained to the old man that he'd soon be moving into a retirement home – "It's a lovely place, Dad... big grounds, beautiful gardens, even has a bowling green" – but Doc's fate went unmentioned. This weekend away, just days before he was due to enter the home, they'd described as a late birthday treat.

"Are we there yet?"

"It's not a joke," Alison warned.

"Perhaps," said Marcie, "he's paying us back for all the times we used to ask him the same question."

"Are we there yet?" he repeated, crossly.

"Not yet, Dad. Not too far, now."

"Doc's going well, isn't he?"

"He always does, Dad," agreed Tim.

"Never lets us down."

"Never has."

They reached the caravan site, half a mile outside Bakewell, just before lunchtime. Their father's memory seemed to have returned, and as they slowly walked into the town, he was recalling previous visits.

"Why didn't you tell me we were coming here? The Blue John Mines at Castleton – you loved it, going underground in those small boats. The fairground at Matlock – we went there a few times. And Hardwick Hall, and Haddon Hall. Chatsworth, of course. Your mother used to say it was the most perfect house in England."

He broke off, his discomfiture obvious.

"Where is she, by the way. You didn't leave her behind, did you?"

"Oh, she's around somewhere," said Alison. "Don't worry. What about the puddings? You've forgotten them."

"Puddings?" He looked up, sharply. "What the bloody hell are you talking about?"

"You know," she said. "Bakewell pudding? The competitions we had?"

"Three shops, Dad," said Tim. "They all claim to have the original recipe. We buy one from each, and vote for our favourite."

"Oh, that. Yes, of course I remember. Why would you think I'd forget that? It's Bakewell pudding, by the way. Not Bakewell tart."

"That's right. We thought we'd do it again. Now. Is that OK with you?"

They bought the three puddings – overly sweet concoctions of custard, ground almonds and jam, baked in a circular pastry base – and found a bench in the recreation ground.

"Well, what's the verdict?" asked Marcie.

"The first one," said the old man, crumbs littering his shirt and trousers. "Definitely, the first one."

24

He took a sip of tea from the thermos flask she passed to him.

"You know," he said after a while, "I never told you this… I thought you might think I was silly—"

"We'd never think that, Dad."

"Well… after you'd all left home, when I was in the house, I'd make a flask of tea, like this, take it outside, and sit in Doc, drinking it. It was like being on holiday all over again. It's the taste. And the smell. Petrol. Leather. The plastic flask. Sometimes, your mother would come and join me. She'd make some sandwiches, and we'd just sit there, having our lunch, our tea…"

"We could do that today, if you like."

"We'll ask your mother, when she gets here. You know, I'd like to go back and sit in him for a while, now. I know you won't let me drive him, and I understand why. It's because… it's because… I'm not as good a driver as I was. I was a good driver, wasn't I?" he asked urgently, tears welling up in his eyes.

"Course you were, Dad. The best. You and Doc."

"Yes. Thanks, son. But, for now, I'd just like to sit in the driving seat. Put my hands on the wheel. Pretend. Would that be alright?"

"That'd be fine. Whatever you want. It's your treat, after all."

"And then when your mother arrives, maybe she'll sit next to me?"

"I'm sure she will."

The doctor had warned them that their father's deterioration might suddenly accelerate, and that his inability to complete routine tasks and make decisions would become obvious.

"At times he'll understand what's happening to him, at other times he won't," she'd told them. "He'll find it hard to distinguish between what's real and what isn't. He may imagine things and people. His dependence on others will increase: he might start to follow you around, repeat things, ask you the same questions over and over again, accuse you of things you haven't done, threaten you. It's important to remain non-judgmental. Try not to get into an argument with him. Be gentle with him, just as you would with a child. I'd be lying if I tried to tell you it won't be stressful, difficult, for you. It will."

When their father, tired by the day's activities, fell asleep in one of Doc's four bunk-beds, the three of them sat outside on folding chairs, sharing a bottle of wine, watching and listening to the sights and sounds of the numerous children playing around the other caravans and tents.

"Well, today's gone quite well," said Alison.

"Yes, it has," agreed Marcie. "But – it's like you said before – he's so old. I don't think I'd realised how much of who he was is slipping away. Shakespeare got it, didn't he – second childhood, mere oblivion?"

"It comes and goes. That's the problem. A lot of the time, he's quite lucid, quite reasonable. Then he'll suddenly say or do something out of the blue, and he's another person."

"We worry about him," said Tim. "Do you think he still worries about us?"

"What do you mean?"

"Well, look at the three of us. Five marriages between us, seven children—"

"And four stepchildren," added Alison.

"Yeah. A mixed bunch. Whereas he and Mum were always so… constant. No disruptions, no upheavals. They must have hoped for the same for us. The same certainties, the same sense of permanence. They never criticised, never interfered. But they must have worried."

26

Tim stood up to return a stray football to half a dozen boys and girls who'd got together for an impromptu game. Two young children, watched over by their father, were paddling in the stream. A teenage girl was dancing blissfully to some imagined music. At the next caravan, a game of hide-and-seek was being organised.

"Forty years ago, that was us," said Marcie.

"Would you go back?"

"In a heartbeat."

When they awoke the next morning, his bed was empty.

"He won't have gone far," said Alison. "I'll stay here in case he comes back. You two go and look for him."

They found him on his knees under the fourteenth-century arched stone bridge over the River Wye, at the northern edge of the town. He was desperately searching for something in the long grass.

"You OK, Dad?" asked Tim.

"Some bugger's only gone and stolen my wallet! I've got an idea it might be round here somewhere." He looked up suspiciously. "It wasn't one of you, was it?"

Marcie helped him to his feet.

"Here it is, Dad," she said, pulling it from his shirt pocket. "You must have forgotten you'd put it there."

"Give it to me!" he demanded, snatching it out of her hand. "And take your bloody hands off me! What the hell's going on? What are you playing at? Do you think I'm bloody stupid? Is this some kind of trick? It's not the only thing that's gone missing, you know. There's somebody comes into the house when I'm not there. Hides under the bed or in a cupboard. I've told you before, but no one listens to me. A Polish fellow. Or an Albanian. Moves things around, steals things. I reckon he's followed us here… Hey, you!" he shouted, suddenly catching sight of a cyclist on the bridge above them. He turned to Tim in fury. "That's him, son! I'm telling you, that's him! Acting like he doesn't hear us! Getting away on his bike! Aren't you going to stop him? Bloody thief!"

"That's a good start to the day," commented Alison, when they arrived back at the caravan site. "What if he'd got himself lost? Or fallen into the river?"

"He's OK. And we can't very well keep him locked up."

"And the retirement home?"

"He has to tell them whenever he goes out. And they have cameras, monitors."

"He'll hate it."

"There's no alternative," said Marcie. "Not after this morning's episode. If we hadn't been there, I think he'd have attacked that poor cyclist."

"He'll be alright. And we'll all visit whenever we can."

"With the children?"

"Of course. Although the last time he saw Jack, he didn't recognise him. Told him to clear off back to the Falkland Islands!"

"The Falkland Islands?"

"I've no idea."

"It does have its comical moments," smiled Tim. "It's hard not to laugh sometimes."

"And hard not to cry at other times," added Marcie.

In the afternoon, they drove to Chesterfield. They stood in the churchyard of St Mary & All Saints, gazing upward at its famed crooked spire, bizarrely twisting and leaning round on itself.

"Thirteenth century, you know," said their father. "Well, the church is. The spire was added a hundred years later. That was the problem: they used unseasoned wood – easier to work with, you see – so of course it was always going to warp. And then they added lead sheeting which was much too heavy for the timber frame to support. That made it even worse. It's not the only one. There are a couple in Devon, and lots in France, in The Loire, for some reason. Don't know why. But this is the best."

He saw them staring at him.

"What's the matter?"

"How do you know all that, Dad?" asked Alison. "That's fantastic."

"I like that!" he said in mock anger. "I'm not entirely senile. Not yet. Which reminds me: anyone seen my Zimmer frame?"

He wandered into the church, still grinning.

"That was amazing," breathed Marcie. "Just like… just like I remember him."

"They're still there," Tim said. "His sense of humour, all the things he used to know, all the things he used to talk about. It's just that it's getting harder for him to access them."

"Well, if nothing else, the weekend will have been worth it for that alone," Alison declared. "That's the first time I've seen him smiling, laughing, happy again, in ages. Let's hope it lasts."

Knowing that the aroma of fish and chips would never be allowed to pollute Doc's pristine interior, Tim fetched them from Bakewell on a bike borrowed from the site office. They ate them sitting outside, as they had done the previous evening. The old man had barely spoken on the drive back from Chesterfield, responding to their questions with occasional nods and shrugs. Now he was slumped listlessly in his chair, his meal forgotten.

"Good day, Dad?" Tim asked.

"Not bad."

29

"Sunday tomorrow. Our last day. What would you like to do?"

"Can we go to Chesterfield? The crooked spire? I've always wanted to see it."

"Dad, we've—" began Marcie.

"We can if you want to," Tim intervened. "Anywhere else?"

"What about Dovedale?" suggested Alison. "You know, the stepping stones. Where Marcie got too scared to move when she was halfway across, and was stuck and started shouting for help, and held everyone up, and you had to wade out to bring her back."

"Don't remind me," said Marcie.

"Was that Marcie? Little Marcie? Was that… I thought it was… I thought… I…"

He looked at Marcie in bewilderment and began to weep. Softly, at first, like the whimpering of a puppy, but soon the sobs gave way to real tears, and cries – hopeless, helpless cries – of pain and rage and sorrow and regret. They stood around him, hiding him, holding his hands in theirs, protecting him from the frightened glances of the children and the concerned stares of the adults.

"I can't… no… it's not… you don't…"

"It's OK, Dad. We're here. Don't worry. It's OK."

They helped him into his bunk and when he was asleep, they came outside again.

"That was awful," Marcie said. "Is that what it's going to be like from now on?"

"When does he go into the home?" asked Alison.

"Wednesday."

"I can stay with him until then. I don't think we should leave him on his own."

"Right. And then we ought to make a start on clearing the house. As soon as we can."

"And Doc?"

"Dad's not asked, so I haven't said anything. The buyer's coming to collect him next weekend. Coming from Cardiff. Chap called Carnaby."

"Like the street?"

"Like the street."

"He must be very keen. To come all that way."

"He is," said Tim. "When he first rang me, I explained the situation, I sent him some photos of Doc, and he offered me the full price immediately."

"Well, I suppose it's for the best."

"I suppose it is."

In the morning, the old man was calm, even subdued.

"This weekend's taken it out of me. I'm not as young as I was, you know. What I'd really like to do is just go for a quiet stroll along the river. Might bump into old Frankie. He lives around here, you know."

"Who's Frankie?" asked Marcie.

"What's that?"

"Frankie. Who is he?"

"You've lost me, love," he said, puzzled. "I don't know anyone called Frankie."

Tim spoke up quickly.

"Yes, let's go down to the river. I think we'd all like that."

"Come on, then. And after that, we'd better get off home. Your mother will be wondering what's happened to us."

For much of the journey back, the old man sat peacefully, saying little, staring fixedly through the windscreen as if he were the driver.

"Doc didn't let us down, did he?" he said, as they neared home.

"No. He never has."

"No, that's right. What's going to happen to him?"

Marcie and Alison sat upright and waited for Tim to answer their father.

"How do you mean, Dad?"

"When I go into this home. What about Doc? What'll happen to him?"

"What would you like to happen?"

"I've been thinking about it. I want you to sell him."

"Sell him? I'm surprised to hear you say that."

"I'm surprised to hear myself say that. More than fifty years, we've had him. Half a century. Taken us everywhere and back again. He watched you grow up, you might say."

"Don't you mind the idea of him belonging to somebody else, Dad?" Alison asked.

"There is that," he said slowly. "Just make sure he goes somewhere where they'll take good care of him, look after him properly. He's not ready for the junkyard yet. Not by a long way. Even if I…"

"Even if nothing, Dad."

"Yes, well. I know you've all been worried about what to do, what to tell me." He noted their surprise. "I told you, I'm not quite senile yet. So, there you are. You can stop worrying. Put your minds at rest. Go ahead and sell him."

"If that's what you want."

"It's what has to be. Now, let's get home. I imagine your mother will have tea ready for us."

While his sisters carried their father's luggage into the house, Tim backed Doc carefully into the garage, and took a long look at him. Still immaculate. The next time he drove out of here, he'd be on the road to Cardiff. A new owner. New roads, new destinations. New passengers, new adventures. A new home. A new life. An old life left behind. He walked slowly into the house, where Marcie called him into the kitchen.

"Alison's taken Dad upstairs to put his things away. They'll be down soon. I'm making tea for us."

"OK. I must just make a phone call."

She heard him from the next room.

"Mr Carnaby. Yes, Tim Fletcher here. That's right. Fine, thanks. How are you? Now – about the Dormobile… I'm afraid I have some bad news."

About the author

Ian Inglis was born in Stoke-on-Trent and now lives in Newcastle upon Tyne. As Reader in Sociology and Visiting Fellow at Northumbria University, he has written several books and many articles around topics within popular culture. He is also a writer of short fiction, and his stories have appeared in numerous anthologies and literary magazines in the UK and US, including *Prole, Popshot, Litro, The Pomegranate, Sentinel Literary Quarterly, Riptide, East Of The Web, The Frogmore Papers,* and *Bandit Fiction.* His debut collection of short stories *The Day Chuck Berry Died* was published by Bridge House in 2023.

Far from the Poppy Fields

Gillian Brown

I never expected to spend my fifteenth birthday like this. Alone in a strange room in an unfamiliar place, with no family or friends to share it with.

I catch my reflection in the mirror. Short back and sides, piled high on top. The current trend. I need to fit in. The problem is the cut accentuates my worst features. A sudden grin cracks my face as I remember my brother calling me Broccoli Ears. I smother the memory and slump onto the bed. My mother's dark eyes appear from nowhere. Guilt swallows me up.

There is a knock at the door. That'll be my social worker. Martin speaks Farsi, but we use English as I need to practise. He sits on the only chair. His build is small, but his presence fills the room. I sit up on the bed and pick at my thumbnail, as his gaze burrows under my skin.

"How's it going today, Ghorban?" he says in his funny accent. It is nothing like the English I learnt at school back home, but I'm getting used to it.

I stare at my feet in their scuffed trainers. "I'm okay."

He laughs, throwing his head back. "Doesn't sound like it."

Raindrops run like black ink down the windowpane. My mood dives further. I remember the heat, dust and beauty of my homeland. Mama is steaming rice on the stove. Through the open doorway, poppies sway in the fields. Beyond them, mountains. I swipe a tear from my cheek.

"It's been weeks," I say, tapping my fingers on my knee. "I want to go to school. College. Become British. Nothing ever happens." I've told Martin this a thousand times. This room is like a prison. I should have stayed in Afghanistan.

"Hey. Slow down. Have you any idea how many asylum seekers there are? New arrivals are escalating. Every week, new wars break out. More repressive regimes gain power. It's complicated, but you've already made progress. You've been granted refugee status. It takes time."

A heavy sigh escapes me. Same old. Same old.

"You must have patience." Martin's face brightens. "Besides, I've some good news! You start secondary school in September."

I stifle a burst of joy, then offer a shrug. "Everyone gets that."

"Perhaps, but it's a positive step forward. You should be pleased, Ghorban."

I open my mouth to speak but nothing comes out.

Martin clears his throat. "Is something else troubling you?"

"I'm tired. It's hard to sleep." I squirm under his scrutiny as the nightmares rush back. The recurring dream about the boy who fell overboard in a storm off Greece. He screamed for help. We didn't stop. His cries grew fainter until the boat's engine finally drowned them out. Some nights his scream gets so loud it wakes me up. I lie there staring into the dark till morning.

"Are you taking your medication?"

"No."

"It will help you sleep."

"I don't want pills. I want my settlement application accepted." I punch my mattress. "I don't exist. I belong nowhere!"

Martin looks away, his Adam's apple bobbing up and down. "We're getting there," he says, like a robot again. "Your case is complex." He throws me an apologetic smile. "This is a long, tedious process."

I clench and unclench my fists.

Martin folds his arms. "I'm here to help you. Please understand that."

I scan his face. It may be true. But my blood is boiling. Anger tears up my throat and bursts out before I can stop it. "I'll start a riot! I don't care if they throw me out of my lodging. I'll do anything to catch attention. This immigration system is rubbish." I pause to catch my breath, then drop my voice to a mutter. "I wish I'd been blown up with the same bomb that killed my father."

"What did you say?"

"You heard me."

His eyes blaze. "Have you forgotten the 12,000 kilometres of hell you went through to get here? Hidden in lorries, hardly able to breathe. Jammed into overcrowded boats, barely seaworthy. The anxiety. The hunger. The loneliness. All that hardship and you can talk like that?"

"Yes."

"No, Ghorban! This is about *you*. It's *your* future. It's what you dreamed of."

"Nobody cares."

"That's not true." Martin stands up and paces three steps across my tiny room. Three steps back again. He shakes his head, rubbing his brow. "It's frustrating, I know. Paperwork... more paperwork." He sighs. "I'll speak to the senior caseworker. See if we can speed things up."

He pulls his chair up close and sits back down again. "Do you ever think of your family?"

Memories swarm in. Mama is crouched down, a knitted shawl around her shoulders as she milks the goats. I'm emptying pails of milk into steel containers to take to market. My brothers are in the poppy fields earning a pitiful few afghanis a day. That was before poppy cultivation was banned. What are they doing now? I've heard many work in brick factories. For women and girls, things are much worse. Poor Mama.

A surge of love fills my chest as I remember Papa and I kite fighting – or playing chess together – before he was killed. My chest deflates. Soon after that, things fell apart. My uncles forced Mama to remarry. My stepfather hated me and threw me out of the house. With a heavy heart, I acted on a tip-off from a friend. I sneaked through the border to Pakistan and stowed away on a migrant boat.

Martin's voice interrupts my thoughts. "Your family are part of your identity, Ghorban. Your own flesh and blood. Have you kept in touch?"

"No."

"Why not?"

A knife tears at my insides as it does every time I think of it. "I left without telling my mother. Now I'm too ashamed to speak to her." My heart cramps up. "I had no choice. She'd only have stopped me."

"A difficult decision. Understandable. But you could contact her now." He looks at his watch. His time is up. "At least, consider it."

Later, I turn Martin's idea over in my head a hundred times. The more I think about it, the more impossible it becomes. What can I say to her? I need to prove myself first. Justify my leaving. But Martin is right. My past is as much a part of me as my future. This truth calms the storm in my head a little. Gives me strength.

The morning before my first day at school, I let out my suppressed joy and dance around the room, whooping. I want to call Mama but I don't. When Martin arrives, my excitement is contagious. We punch fists till my knuckles hurt. "Now we're getting somewhere," he says.

Standing back, he fiddles with a button on his shirt. "You'll be bullied at school, you know. Expect racist comments." I don't care if they beat me up or spit on me. It's a start. "Speaking good English will help. Just be warned."

He is right. Insults are hurled as fast and sharp as Grandpa's old hunting knife. I ignore them until one cuts too deep. "Son of a whore!" I reach out with my fist but the guy is too big and too quick. He knocks me down and pins me to the floor. "Sod off back to where you belong!" He kicks me and runs off with his mates, laughing.

Bruised inside and out, I struggle to my feet. I am not welcome. I should never have come. A memory floods back. Fields of mauve and pink poppies flash before me. They bend double in the wind. Fierce gusts tear at their delicate petals. They shiver and shake but miraculously cling on.

I mustn't give up. I breathe new fire into my lungs. I cut down on my fitness routine, and study all my free time. I remind myself I'm doing this for Mama as much as for myself. The sooner I can earn money, the sooner I can help her. There is Martin too. I don't want to let him down.

Things improve for a while. My classmates find someone new to pick on. Ben becomes my best friend. Or so I think, until the day he stands up in front of the class before the teacher arrives and says, "I'm never speaking to Ghorban again."

As Ben avoids eye contact, I notice dark bruises on his face and neck. These bullies could seriously harm him. Or worse. I must let him go. A void opens up inside me. Their hatred rushes in. I've never felt more alone. I run from the room, slamming the door behind me.

That same night, I gather the savings I've made from odd jobs around the place and buy a six-pack of extra-strong lager from a man who asks no questions. I've never touched alcohol before. If it kills me, who cares?

The more I drink, the more vivid the images in my head become. I'm playing *Pajpar*, or Five Suits, with Mama. Her work-worn fingers grip the cards. Her brow creases in concentration. A surge of love for her overwhelms me and I let her win the hand. She laughs with such joy that I join in and give her a hug. She strokes my hair. I'm her baby boy again.

I crack open another can. And another. My mind tips. Mama shouts at me. "Why did you leave without telling me?" She slaps my cheek. "Why are you drinking alcohol?" I take another swig. Her features become a blur. Her words muffled.

With the last can, I sink into a pit too deep to crawl out of. My mother will never forgive me. I'll never see her again. My heart breaks into a million pieces, scattering like shards of glass across the floor. I take a last gulp of lager, stagger to the basin and grab my newly bought razor. The world narrows down to a sharp blade and the pulsing vein on my wrist.

I don't remember any pain, just a sudden spurt of blood.

"Luckily, you screamed," Martin tells me later. "The neighbours heard you, and saved your life."

Luckily? I'm not so sure.

Martin helps me get back into a routine. I never touch alcohol again and bury myself in my studies. Days turn into months. Months to years.

My dream finally gets closer. I pass my A' levels. Soon, I'll have my British passport. I'll belong. My heart is still pumping when Martin appears, not long after I receive the results. When he sees my grin, he throws his head back laughing. "Have you won the lottery?"

"I got top grades in my A-levels!" I punch the air in the Anglo-Saxon way. "Yes!"

"Ghorban! Congratulations!" He shakes my hand so hard I think my arm might drop off. His face turns serious. "Have you told your...?" He stops as I avert my gaze. The missing word sits like a ghost on his tongue. A wall of silence stands between us.

Once he is gone, I take several deep breaths. I can't wait any longer. My hand trembles as I grab my phone and punch in the number. It seems to ring forever. An echo from the far side of the world. Then there's a click and a suspicious "Hello". The sound of Mama's voice is as sweet as the *shira pira* dessert she makes to celebrate the poppy harvest. Rich and creamy. My favourite.

Martin returns the next morning. He hands me an official-looking paper. "We're almost there. I need a signature." He laughs. "The last one, I promise!" When I don't respond, he frowns. "Well? Aren't you over the moon?"

It all seems secondary now. "I spoke to my mother."

Martin stifles a gasp. "And?"

"I told her everything." I drop my head to my knees and burst into tears.

"Ghorban? Are you all right?" He lays a hand on my shoulder. "Was she angry?"

I look up. "She said she was proud of me."

About the author
Gillian Brown started out as a travel writer but now concentrates on fiction. Much of her work is still inspired by her travels. She has won the Yeovil Literary Prize and her short stories have been published in various magazines and online. They have also been included in several anthologies: *Bridge House, Westword, Leicester Writes, Write Time, Earlyworks Press* and *Stringybark,* among others. She was born in Scotland and lives in France.

Floored

Fiona Ritchie Walker

"Ow!"

Molly rubbed her head. This was different, seeing her kitchen from floor level. She knew the chair was wobbly. Why stand on it to reach the vase? Now glass shards lay everywhere.

Again Molly tried pulling herself up, then slumped against the wall. Her left leg was bent and pain shot through when she tried to stand. She fumbled for the emergency pendant that she'd reluctantly accepted when moving into the sheltered housing complex. Nothing. Of course, it would be lying on the bedside table, right next to her mobile phone.

"Oh well, I'll just have to yell and hope someone walking down the back lane can hear me," Molly told the empty room. "Why couldn't I fall on a Tuesday when Brenda and Mary would be calling round so we would head off to Knit and Natter together? Here goes."

She took a deep breath. "Help! Help!"

"Crikey, that was enough to wake the dead."

Molly looked up to see a familiar figure by the sink. "Toby! What are you doing here?"

"I'm not sure. How long since I?"

"Three years." Molly stared at her husband. "Is it really you? I must say you're looking better than the last time I saw you."

Toby shook his head. "I did tell you not to go for the open casket."

"Yes, that was a big mistake. Nightmares for weeks afterwards." Molly winced. "Anyway, however you got here and wherever you've come from, there's no way I can give you a welcome hug. I fell off the chair and my leg's agony – won't move."

Toby stretched out his hand towards the kitchen unit, then frowned as his fingers went right through it. "I'm not sure a hug would work. I'm like something out of a magic show, which is annoying as I wanted to open this drawer, get you some paracetamol."

Molly shook her head. "You can't."

"I know, that's the problem with being dead."

"No. You can't because the paracetamol aren't there anymore."

"But we always kept them there."

"They're in the drawer below the tumblers now. Seemed more logical."

"Logical?" Toby looked puzzled. "Best kept beside the sink I'd say. You need water to wash down tablets."

"Capsules, Toby. I use capsules now. Much easier to swallow."

"Capsules? You never complained about the tablets."

"They always got stuck in my throat, although it's ages since I needed one."

"Two, Molly." Toby tried to open the drawer again. "Oh, bother, I was hoping I could read you the instructions."

"No!" Molly shrieked, making Toby jump, or at least rise up slightly.

"I'm sure you probably could take one, Molly, it's just that a dose of two seems to be the norm – or it was when I was alive."

Molly sighed. Was she hallucinating? If so she'd certainly summoned up the real Toby, warts and all. "Typical. I call for help and get my dead husband with a lecture on paracetamol. Oh hell!"

Toby folded his arms, making Molly wonder why one arm didn't dissolve into the other. "I'll have you know Hell is not where I came from."

"Sorry. Wasn't meaning you." Molly pointed at the

radiator. "I put some washing to dry and just spotted my favourite knickers. What with me stuck on the floor and you being, well, you know, there's no chance of moving them before anyone arrives."

Toby made a face. "Do you really wear them?"

"They're comfort fit! And were pale cream until I washed them with brown jeans and they went, well, streaky."

"Oh, a washing malfunction and not you, that's a relief." Toby smiled. "Remember those little French knickers you wore on honeymoon? All satin and soft, tiny too."

"Thank you, Toby. Yes, I remember them very well, a wonderful few days in Parish, and I remember my rather slim reflection in the bathroom mirror. But that was nearly fifty years ago and what I want to know is why no-one's using the back lane this morning?"

Toby floated towards the window and peered out. "Not a soul. Oh, Molly Moo – how could you!"

"What?"

"My cascading flower beds."

Molly pictured the displays Toby had created over the years. "They were wonderful, but I don't like gardening and didn't have time to—"

"Not even a tub. All gravel!" Toby stared. "Is that a…"

"Concrete gnome? Yes, won in a raffle."

Toby tilted his head. "It looks like—"

"You?"

"Certainly not! I was about to say it must have been the booby prize."

Molly's face twisted with pain. "None of this is helping, Toby. Is anyone there?"

"Oh, a séance! Shall we join hands?"

"Toby, you're dead. We can't hold hands. I just want someone alive and able to call an ambulance. Help!" Her voice faded and she closed her eyes.

"Don't fall sleep." Toby moved closer. "I wish I could hold you, like old times. I know, let's play a game. I spy with my little eye…"

"I'm not ten, Toby."

"I could sing."

"Oh, I feel bad enough already."

There was silence and Molly wondered if Toby had gone, then heard his voice again. Or was it in her head?

"Seeing you on the floor reminds me of that night at college."

Molly nodded. "Our second date."

"That terrible storm. We snuggled down on the floor by the fire."

"Oh, Toby, you make it sound romantic, but I nearly singed my hair on those awful electric bars and then the meter ran out." Molly tried to move. "Ouch!"

"I wish I could help."

"You are, just being here. But the pain is so bad." Molly slumped down further onto the floor and rested her head against the wall.

"Morning, Molly."

A different voice! Was this another vision from her past? Molly opened her eyes and looked up as a smiling face appeared around the kitchen door.

"Just me. I wondered if you'd like some eggs – what on earth has happened?"

Molly automatically tried to tidy her unruly hair. Why, oh why did it have to be George?

And there was Toby beside him, glaring.

"Oh, George. I was so stupid. Climbed on a chair and now look at me. I think my leg's broken."

"Right." George threw the box of eggs on the table and pulled a mobile from his pocket. "First thing, ambulance." He squinted at the screen. "Not much of a signal, I'll nip outside into the lane."

"George?" Toby raised his eyebrows, which made him float a little higher.

"Yes, remember he ran the camera shop."

Toby nodded. "And his wife?"

"She died. Not long after you."

"So you and—"

"Me and George?" Molly laughed. "We're neighbours since he moved in to the bungalow a few doors down."

"He seems nice. I don't like to see you on your own, Molly. I mean, climbing on chairs at your age. You need someone to look after you, and if it can't be me…"

"But you said you didn't want me to get married again."

Toby shook his head. "Good grief, Molly. Don't you think you're jumping the gun? He's only brought some eggs!"

"Right." George appeared in the doorway. "Ambulance on its way." He examined his shirt cuff and frowned. "Must have cracked an egg when I put them on the table. Is there an old cloth?"

Molly watched with horror as George pointed at her knickers on the radiator.

"Ah, perfect!" He turned on the tap. "Don't worry, I'll rinse this out afterwards."

"No, you can't!" Molly blurted out.

George held up the knickers. "What's wrong with this rag?"

"Oh, well, it's just, what I mean is," Molly swallowed hard. "What I meant is there are much nicer rags in the drawer."

George laughed. "Nicer rags, that's a good one." He began dabbing his cuff. "This'll do."

Molly held her breath. Any moment now George would realise he was cleaning his beautiful shirt not with a kitchen rag, but a pair of brown-stained knickers. Her knickers. He'd never visit again. Even worse, if he told others, she'd be known as the knicker lady and have to move. But where? Molly's mind raced ahead until she realised George had draped her undies over the tap and was walking towards her.

"I remember, from a first aid course many moons ago, that I need to keep you warm." Molly could smell George's aftershave as he draped the jacket around her.

"Oh, that feels good," she murmured, letting her head lean on his shoulder. Then, realising what she was doing, Molly jolted up and looked at Toby. With a smile, he blew her a kiss, then disappeared.

"Toby!" Molly called out.

George patted her shoulder. "Sadly, I'm not Toby, but I do want to make sure you're OK."

"He was here, in the kitchen." Molly sighed. "Or maybe my brain just invented him so I wouldn't be alone." She yawned. "How much longer?"

George checked his watch. "Should be just a few minutes. But don't fall asleep on the floor or you'll ache in the morning."

Molly tried to sit upright. "Sounds like you're speaking from experience."

"When my wife was in hospital, the night duty nurse was so kind, turning a blind eye when I sneaked back in to sleep by her bed."

Molly looked at him. "It's tough, isn't it."

"Absolutely," George said, his eyes glistening. "You're left with such a big hole in your life. Goodness knows what I'd do without Lottie and Lulu." He looked thoughtful. "You know, Molly, I think you'd all get on really well. Yes, once you're better I should introduce you."

Molly stiffened. "Why would I want to meet your… companions?"

George laughed. "Hens actually, on the allotment. Laying like mad, which is why I thought I'd bring some round." A guilty look crossed his face. "Well, I do have an ulterior motive."

"Really?"

"Yes. I wondered if you—" He took a deep breath. "If you'd agree to—"

Molly began nodding. Yes, dinner or a coffee, maybe a walk by the river. Any of these would be wonderful, when she was back on both legs of course.

"I've been reinforcing the girls' run, because of the foxes. Could I borrow your hideous garden gnome to frighten them off?"

Molly kept nodding. Why on earth had she thought he'd invite her out? And where was the ambulance? Suddenly she felt exhausted and her eyelids drooped.

"I know, what about a game to keep you awake?"

"Oh, George, please not I spy!"

"Heavens Molly, you're not ten! As we're at ground level, what about listing all the floors we've ever slept on?"

Molly laughed. "I do remember arriving late at a French campsite with my parents and sister. We put up the tent in the dark. Next morning we heard laughter outside. Turned out we'd slept in the children's play park."

George put his arm round Molly's shoulder. She shivered, but this time with pleasure.

"I slept on a youth hostel floor in Germany when I was a teenager," he said. "My mate and I arrived back late and the door was locked, so we sneaked in through a window. The dorm was pitch black and I couldn't remember which bunk was mine, so ended up sleeping between the beds, fully clothed, with someone's rucksack as a pillow. It was OK until someone climbing down from the top bunk stood on me in the morning."

Before Molly could reply, a face appeared at the door and George was up in a flash, explaining the situation to the paramedic.

Molly looked at the egg box on the table. A cake, yes, soon as she could, as a thank you, with coffee. She knew George would say yes.

"Are you coming to the hospital too?" the paramedic asked George as they wheeled Molly towards the door.

George squeezed Molly's hand. "Absolutely. I'm staying right beside her. Even if I end up on another floor."

About the author
Fiona Ritchie Walker is a Scottish writer of poetry and short fiction, now based in Bournville, Birmingham. Her work has been widely published over the years. In 2024 she won the Scottish Poetry Library's Julia Budenz Scots Poetry Competition, the Neil Gunn Poetry Competition and was among the prizewinners in the Edinburgh Award for Flash Fiction.

Fran's Birthday Party

Veronica Robinson

"A call for you, Miss Henry."

I stepped into the hallway and took the receiver of the payphone from my landlady.

"Hello."

"It's Andrew."

"So you remembered."

"What should I have remembered this time?"

"Your daughter's birthday. I thought that's what this call was about."

"Of course. Did you think I'd forgotten?"

Fran tugged at my skirt. "Come on, Mummy."

"Just a minute Fran, I'm speaking to your daddy."

"Let me speak to Daddy. Mummy, let me speak."

"Okay. Just say hello."

"Hello, Daddy."

"Hello, sweetie. I will see you later."

I took the phone. "We've got to go."

"What time are you in later?"

"About five."

"I'll be there at six."

"Fran's bedtime is seven. I need to get her settled because she's having a little party tomorrow."

"No problem. I will see you later."

Fran and I hurried to the bus stop.

"I wish Daddy didn't live in France. I wished he lived here. He could take me to school sometimes and I wouldn't always be late."

"I'm sorry, Fran, I will try to be early next time."

"I always miss assembly."

"Let's hurry."

The auditorium was empty, so I knew that assembly was over and all the children were in their classes.

"Go on to your class Fran. Mummy has to leave."

"Miss Dent will be cross."

"No she won't. We're just a little late."

"She'll still be cross."

"If you don't go in now she'll really be cross."

Fran began to cry.

"What's the trouble?" said Mr Patterson coming into the auditorium.

"So glad to see you, Mr Patterson, we're a little bit late, and Fran is afraid of upsetting her teacher."

"Don't be upset, Fran. I will sort it out."

"Thanks, Mr Patterson. I've got to rush."

I ran to the tube station. It was 9:30am. I was due at Broadcasting House at 10:30am.

"I see you're early," Thomas James said.

"Ten minutes to go. Edna will be pleased."

"Man, if you weren't on time today, I don't think she would want to work with you again."

Edna Davies was our radio producer.

"She's so understanding."

"Lights on,' whispered Thomas. And we started to record.

At lunchtime, Edna rode with me and Thomas in the elevator to the canteen.

"I'm seeing Courtney Jones for lunch, to talk about his new play. It's set in today's multiracial Britain. A bi-racial couple and their mixed-race family. We are thinking of doing a series."

"That's the best news I've heard all week," said Thomas. "A multiracial series means steady work for a multiracial cast."

"I just hope I get a part."

"The series could be based on you, Vie, with Andrew and Fran. Maybe Courtney Jones could speak to you about it."

"My set up is not the best example of family life. But it would be interesting to hear what Fran had to say."

We came out of the lift and went our separate ways. Edna to meet Courtney Jones, Thomas and I to eat lunch together.

"It's a nice afternoon. We could go for a walk in the park, then back to my place, and I could cook you a meal later. Relax. Have some fun."

"Sorry, Thomas. I have to rush home, do some housework. Get some extra shopping done. It's Fran's birthday tomorrow. I have to pick her up from school, and if that's not enough, her father is visiting."

"How's Fran reacting?"

"She hasn't seen him yet. She just said hello on the phone."

"I hope this means he's bucking up his act."

"There's nothing I can say to him that will make his visits less erratic."

"I knew something was going on when you kept turning up late for recordings."

"Things are getting to me a bit. I'm tired of chasing him up over his financial contributions. I can't sleep at night, and I drift off in the mornings when I should get up, and it throws a wrench in my routine."

"Don't let things get to you, Vie. If you need any help to get through the weekend, let me know."

"I might take you up on that. Knowing how unreliable he can be, maybe I should just let Fran take potluck on seeing him, and not build up her hopes."

51

"You're only human, Vie, you can't always know the best thing to do. By the way, I got Fran a little something for her birthday."

"You remembered. How sweet. Andrew might not show, so why don't you come over about four tomorrow."

I knew something was wrong the moment I entered the auditorium. Mr Patterson usually jovial, and with a smile for me, was glum.

"Fran?"

"Upstairs with Mrs Patterson."

"Can I go up?"

"She is expecting you."

Mrs Patterson did not look too upset. That was a relief. But the mother of Fran's best friend Shirley, Mrs Kaye, was visibly shaken. I held my breath.

"The police were here. You just missed them," said Mrs Patterson.

I was silent.

"Fran and Shirley went missing."

"During class?"

"After school."

I looked at Fran. She was concentrating on her shoes.

"Fran told Shirley she wanted to get home to see her father," said Mrs Kaye. "They boarded a bus and when they couldn't pay the fare, the conductor realised they were on their own. She alerted the driver and they dropped them off at the police station down the road."

"But you know you should wait for me, Fran."

"You're always late."

"I'm sorry," said Mrs Kaye. "But Fran is a bad influence. Shirley won't be at her party tomorrow."

"The important thing is they are both safe and well," said Mrs Patterson. She turned to me. "We need to have a further talk about Fran. Perhaps you could get her father to join us. Fran says he's visiting."

"I will try."

"It's nine. Fran went to bed hours ago."

"Sorry. I got side tracked with some colleagues. We went for a drink and the time just flew by."

"You didn't come for her birthday did you?"

"Actually, I'm just passing through. I'm on my way to cover the war in Biafra. But I did think of Fran. I'm here. You can't accuse me of not caring."

"You have a funny way of showing it. I haven't had a penny from you for childcare in four months. And you haven't got a present for her birthday, have you?"

"I'll make it up to her tomorrow."

"You're impossible, you know that."

"Mummy, look what I've got."

"It's lovely, Fran. Whose idea was it to get a black board?"

"Mine."

"I took her to Hamleys. She didn't want a doll, she wanted this blackboard."

"I can teach Daddy how to do sums."

"Daddy has to leave early, sweetie," said Andrew. "You can teach me another time."

"You mean you won't be at my party?"

"Sorry, sweetie, Daddy has an important job to do."

"I've got to have a private talk with you, Andrew. It concerns Fran."

"I just don't have the time, Vie. It will have to wait."

"Of course. You are always too busy."

"Don't start."

"Hello, hello. Am I in time for the party?"

"Thomas, your timing is perfect. Andrew was just leaving."

53

"You didn't tell me Thomas was invited."

"I didn't know you would be here."

"I brought Fran a Caribbean rag doll. Hope she likes it," said Thomas.

"She'll be over the moon," I said.

Andrew gave Thomas a challenging look. "I took her to Hamleys this morning, she wasn't interested in any of the dolls."

"You know what women are like Andrew. Maybe she will have a change of heart."

"Look, Fran, Uncle Thomas got you a doll."

"Thanks, Uncle Thomas. I can teach her sums."

"Fran, give Daddy a kiss. I've got to go."

"When are you coming back?"

"As soon as I can."

"Before my next birthday?"

"Long before your next birthday."

"I will be six."

"I know. You'll soon be grown up."

"Are you going to give Mummy a kiss?"

"Uncle Thomas can do that. I've got a war to cover."

After saying goodbye to Andrew. I saw the two kids from next door playing in their front yard. They were a bit older than Fran. Seven and eight, but they often played hopscotch with her on the pavement outside.

"Hello, Girls. Ask your mum if you can come in, and share Fran's birthday cake and ice cream. Her daddy had to leave suddenly, and there is more than enough for two."

"Yes please," they said. "We'd love to come."

As Fran demonstrated how to add and subtract on her blackboard, I sat at the back of the room with Thomas and quietly enjoyed the party that nearly did not happen.

About the author

Veronica Robinson is Jamaican/British. She started writing in Jamaica for the evening newspaper, producing stories, articles and an advice column. She also contributed in two short films and a flash fiction story to *City Lit* magazine, "Between The Line". For the past ten years, Veronica has been attending a writers' group focusing on writing short stories and flash fiction. Recently she has had eleven stories published.

Helping Angel

Peter Collins

Her name was Angel. I remember because she was my very first client in my new job. I'm not sure quite what to tell you about my job; it's a bit hard to describe. Gabe says we're here to spread the good news; he talks like that sometimes. Gabe's my supervisor. He's been in the job forever; though to be fair, you wouldn't know it to look at him. He's in real good shape. He's way older than me, but I wouldn't fancy taking him on. I suppose things were different back then when the operation started; tougher times than they are now.

Basically, our job is to protect people; people we've never even heard of. The boss hands down a list of names and we have to look after them. You've probably heard of the boss. He's the top man in the justice department. El Numero Uno. Not that I have much to do with him at my level. I've only met him once when I started. It was the usual routine: firm handshake, penetrating look in the eyes, welcome to the team, learn from Gabe, he's the best; all that corporate stuff. But it was different in a way, kind of inspiring if you know what I mean. I've never been much of a company man. I saw way too much brown nosing back in my days on the force. But this guy wasn't like that; what he was doing was awesome in a way. I didn't say anything, of course, just nodded, but it felt good working for him.

Some assignments were long-term; Gabe told me of a few he'd worked on for years. But as a new boy, I'd only be given short-term jobs. Like a kind of probation until I won my wings, sort of stuff. I don't want to sound cocky, but I was pretty confident I could handle it. You see, back in the day, I was a cop, and a pretty good one at that. But that all stopped on the day we got called to a robbery and I took a bullet in the chest. I knew there and then that was me out of the force. They don't like keeping cops who have been shot. It's like a reminder to everybody else that it might be their turn next time. They paid out the pension right enough and my kid still keeps the medal they gave me, but it was the end of my police career.

That's sort of how I ended up here, I suppose. When one of the boss' guys asked me if I fancied giving it a go, I pretty much jumped at the chance: excitement, action – I'm in. And then for my first assignment Gabe tells me I've got to look after a waitress in some small seaside resort I'd never even heard of. He wouldn't even tell me anything about her, apart from her name. Figure it out as you go along, he said. Talk about starting at the bottom.

They hadn't fixed me up with any means of transport, so Gabe dropped me off. It was a cool autumn day and dark clouds were being blown about by a strong breeze. He set me down at a bench overlooking the sea by some ancient cliff-side tramway. The place was quiet apart from a few dog walkers and some hardy OAPs all rugged up against the elements. I expected some last-minute words of encouragement but Gabe just pointed down the hill.

"I'll be here when you've finished," was all he said.

I made my way down the steep steps to the front. The tide was in, and the waves were breaking hard against the pier. A pair of lunatics in wetsuits were trying to manhandle a surfboard into the sea. Just looking at them made me shiver.

The café was easy to find. It was kind of shabby looking, but clean enough. I found a table and looked at the menu. I didn't even notice the waitress until she came to take my order. She had one of those uniforms they all seem to wear in places like this; you know, plain white dress with blue check on the arms, collar and apron. She had long dark hair and she was skinny rather than slim. I guess she was about thirty, but she looked older. She had rings under her eyes and she looked tired – kind of worn out, if you know what I mean. Her name badge had *Angel* on it. I thought that was pretty ironic.

"What'll it be?" Her voice was kind of tired, too.

"Well, seeing as I'm at the seaside, I guess it'll have to be fish and chips. And a big cup of strong black coffee."

Angel just nodded. She went to the counter. There was nobody there and I noticed that she glanced at the unattended till as if she was worried about it being so insecure. She took the order into the kitchen and came straight back with the coffee. She watched with an amused look as I made a show of holding the cup with both hands and smelling the aroma.

"Man, that smells good."

I took a deep gulp and made appreciative noises like I was tasting a fine wine.

"You sure like your coffee, mister."

"You gotta savour the good things, Angel. It lets you know you're really alive."

When she came back with my order a few minutes later I made the same sort of show about smelling the battered fish and smothering my chips with salt and vinegar.

"Your chef's a genius, Angel. Tell him from me."

This time I was rewarded with a real live smile.

"Arnie's been called a lot things, but that's the first time I've heard 'genius'."

I indicated the chair opposite.

"Join me?"

She looked around the empty café. It was clear that nobody would be needing her services for the next few minutes.

"Are you hitting on me?"

I chewed a mouthful of divine fish before replying.

"You're sweet, kid, but I'm old enough to be your father. Besides, I already got me a real woman back home, look." I took out my wallet and pulled out the picture of Stacey and Robert I'd taken on his fourteenth birthday. After a moment's hesitation she sat down and took the picture in both hands.

"She's pretty. Your boy's cute, too." My heart kind of ached when she said that. It was a while since I'd seen them both. I wondered if I'd remember what they looked like without the picture.

"Here. Look at this." She pulled a picture of her own from a pocket in her uniform and pushed it across shyly. It was a boy, maybe five or six years old, looking intently at the camera, taking the whole photography business very seriously.

"Attractive kid. Was his dad good looking?"

She rapped me on the knuckles with a spoon for that, but for the first time I felt her relax. She pulled the picture back and put it carefully in her pocket.

"His dad was good looking, since you ask. But that was about all he had going for him. It's just me and Billy now. We're better off on our own."

The last phrase was said as if it were a sort of mantra, like she'd told herself over and over again in order to believe it to be true.

"You work here long?"

"Just a few weeks." She kept looking round the place in case anybody needed serving, but she needn't have bothered. We were alone apart from the invisible Arnie who hadn't appeared out of the kitchen. "I'm on a trial period. I get paid by the day." Her eyes lingered on the till again. "Tomorrow's my day off."

59

"Well that's gotta be welcome."

She frowned. "No work, no pay." A dark cloud appeared on her face. "I don't think we can get by without any money." She slumped forward, head in her arms for a moment, and when she sat up her eyes were moist.

Boy, she really could do with some good news, but I sure as hell didn't have any. Gabe had only given me enough money for the fish and chips. When I looked up she was staring at the till again and I finally twigged. She wasn't looking to guard it, she was thinking about stealing from it.

"Is Billy a smart kid?" It was all I could think of to say.

Her face lightened for a minute. "Oh yeah. He's really bright. His teachers say he knows maths better than they do. He's designed some sort of telescope that his science teacher can't believe."

"Good for him. A kid can do anything nowadays if he's got a parent who believes in him." I pushed away the empty plate and wiped my fingers on a paper napkin. "But it's a different life if his parents aren't around. Imagine what would happen to a kid like that if his mum went to prison." I stared openly at the till and saw her follow my gaze. "Put in care; nobody to love him or look after him. Nobody to show him right from wrong. Getting mixed up with gangs, in and out of juvenile court, finally prison. Hell of a big risk for twenty or thirty quid."

She let it go then. She fell forward on the table and wept her heart out. When she sat up, her eyes were red, but her stare was defiant.

"You're right, mister. We can get by a bit longer. Thank you." She reached forward and touched my arm, her fingertips just brushing the skin.

I patted her on the shoulder and paid the bill. Outside I sat on a bench and wondered what to do next. I waited in the weak afternoon sunshine for a while until two minibuses pulled up in the car park. The driver of the first one seemed to be looking at some sort of delivery manifest. He shouted out to the second driver.

"This looks like the place."

The other guy nodded and both minibuses emptied. It was a local rugby team. Big guys, loud and boisterous but still friendly. They seemed in a bit of a daze as if they didn't quite know why they were there. They went straight inside the café and I headed along the front. I walked around for a few hours and made it back just in time to see Angel leave the café. I fell into step with her and we plodded slowly up the hill to the town.

"Hey."

"Hey, you too." She looked different; younger somehow.

"Good day?"

"The best. You'll never believe it." Her eyes were glowing with excitement.

"Try me."

"Just after you left, this rugby team came in. They'd just had a practice session and they were starving. They nearly ate the place empty: fish and chips, steaks, burgers; not just the cheap stuff either. We took as much today as we normally make in a week. They told Arnie that the place had been recommended to them because of a fantastic waitress."

I put on a puzzled expression and she punched me in the arm.

"They meant me, dumbass."

I smiled back at her. "Well good for you."

"Yeah. But I don't understand it. I mean, I've only been there a couple of weeks and I've not exactly been the life and soul of the place. Who'd recommend a café just because of me?"

"Well don't knock it. Luck? Fate? Divine intervention? Who knows?"

"Yeah, well anyway they told Arnie they'd be here twice a week after practice as long as I was still here. Well what could he do? He made me permanent and gave me a rise. It's not a lot, but it all helps." She was practically glowing with excitement.

"I owe you, mister. I dread to think what I might have done if we hadn't had that chat today. Thank you." She leaned across and kissed me on the cheek. We reached the top of the hill and she crossed the road into the town. I watched her walk away for a while and then I headed back to the bench. True to his word, Gabe was sitting there. I shrugged and sat down. It was a while before he spoke.

"You did good, kid."

I looked across at him. Close up, you could really see the signs of age in his face, like he'd seen more of the world than he really wanted to.

"The rugby team was your idea of good news?" I asked.

He smiled. "Call it a helping hand."

I held my head in my hands for a moment. "I don't know if I'm cut out for this, Gabe."

He nodded. "Remembering your wife and son?"

I said nothing.

"You see, kid, that's just the way it is. You quit this job, go back to where you were before and you'll feel fine. You know what it's like there; it's easy to forget your pain and your loss. But this job gives you a chance to make amends. These people need our help. But that help comes at a price – you're still going to feel your old pain.'

"Is Angel's kid going to be someone special?"

"The boss thinks he can do more good for mankind than any twenty scientists put together, as long as his mum keeps him on the straight and narrow. That's why we were sent to help her. Thanks to you she's probably going to do that."

I sat quietly for a moment. Unthinkingly, I ran my finger across the bullet scar on my chest, directly over my heart. On the face of it, a life with no painful memories sounded heavenly, but I knew it wasn't really living. I nodded.

"OK, Gabe. I'm in."

He clapped me on the back and stood up. He shrugged off his jacket and put out a hand. "Hold on." I did as I was told. With a single graceful movement he eased himself forward as his wings uncoiled from his back. He gave a slight shake and they unfurled with a magnificent swishing sound. They gave one huge beat and I held on tight as we were suddenly soaring higher and higher.

I was pleased I'd helped spread a bit of good news today, but I'd not earned my wings yet. But one day, maybe soon, I'd be fully fledged and become a proper Guardian Angel, just like Gabriel.

About the author
Peter is a writer specialising in short stories. He has had over twenty stories published in hard copy anthologies and many more published online. His writing often features a quirky sense of humour and an unexpected twist. He has won a number of prizes for his writing and in 2021 was awarded the HG Wells Fiction Prize. He lives in Leeds, England and when not writing is often out in the Yorkshire countryside either cycling or walking his dog, Saski.

Hero

Mike Wilson

He's meeting Cathy at the usual place, a cosy upscale restaurant in the town where *she* lives, twenty minutes away from the town where *he* lives. The maître-de smiles and nods when he walks in. By now, everyone working there knows who he is. Perhaps they've figured out the rest of it, too.

He navigates between tables to the back corner booth. She has her usual glass of Sauvignon Blanc in front of her and she's ordered one for him, even though he prefers red. He slides in across from her.

"Hey." Her eyes desire him, not big crashing waves of desire, just little ripples lapping the shore that will become big ones if he gives a push. The ocean in Cathy's eyes, he tells himself, eventually will become a stagnant pond, like Diana's if he doesn't break it off. He doesn't believe his own bullshit, but sometimes you tell yourself things because you need them to be true. She's studying his face.

"Are you okay?"

Is she that good at reading him? Because he's weighing up the idea of dumping her. It's a card every married man keeps up his sleeve.

"Just things on my mind." He'll enjoy the evening, then text her tomorrow.

"Me, too."

She has things on *her* mind. Good, the spotlight's not on him. And what could a girl her age have on her mind that matters? He picks up his glass of wine.

"Cheers." They clink glasses.

She's looking out the window. He assumes she's thinking, or whatever passes for thinking in that head of hers. Wait – is she looking for someone? Did Diana follow him?

"Do you see something out there?"

She turns to him, gives him a searching look. "Like what?"

"I don't know." He lifts his glass to his lips and sips. He looks out the window. Nothing there.

"I saw Diana's tennis team won a tournament."

Cathy stalks him on social media, where she's a friend hidden among hundreds, never posting comments – it would call attention to her, prompt Diana to ask *How do you know her?*

"Did you take Diana out to dinner to celebrate?"

She's baiting him to bad-mouth his marriage. She wants to hear the words *divorce papers.* He's too old to fall for it. He maintains control of their conversations like a lion-tamer makes the lioness jump on and off the box at the circus.

"You two ready to order?"

You two. It's Missy, their regular waitress, a big smile on her face. He never knows if Missy's smile is tied to the big tips he leaves or if she's embracing the role of co-conspirator, blessing this older man/younger woman thing like a voyeur vicariously enjoying it. Missy's pen is poised over her pad. He imagines telling her *She'll have a free meal and I'll have sex the way I used to have it in college.*

"House salad," Cathy says. "Hold the onion."

"Beef stroganoff," he says. They hand the menus back to Missy. Cathy points at her half-full wine glass.

"Could you bring me another?"

"Sure." Missy turns to him. "You too?"

His glass is nearly full, but Cathy is more quickly compliant when she's drunk, so he should get on board.

"Yes."

Missy leaves, and Cathy pushes her glass toward him. "Finish mine, will you?"

He looks at the two glasses of wine in front of him, confused. "Why did you order more, if you didn't drink what you had?"

"I just feel like celebrating—"

He doesn't. Diana got into his phone last night, found the sext from Cathy that he couldn't bring himself to delete, and has given him an ultimatum – Diana or the girlfriend. He can't have both.

"—but I really shouldn't have that second glass."

This doesn't sound like Cathy. Cathy *loves* to drink. And she just said she felt like celebrating, though she didn't say why.

"Is this some kind of health kick?"

"They say one glass a day is okay, but more than that, maybe not."

"Who says that?"

"My obstetrician."

Time suddenly slows, and space contracts as if this table is the only place in the universe.

"You're pregnant?"

She nods. "How do you feel about that?"

Holy shit is how he feels about that.

"Here you go!"

It's Missy, setting plates on the table.

"Thank you, I'm starving!" Cathy's cheeks are glowing. He wonders if it's the wine or the pregnancy.

During dinner, Cathy talks about this and that and he barely hears anything she says. But eventually, she circles back to the baby.

"It's a lot to take in. It changes my life." She spears a piece of lettuce with her fork. He thinks about the little organism inside her she's feeding. "I know it's a surprise for you. You don't have to say anything. I'm still thinking about it, too."

He doesn't interrogate her. They never used condoms, but he assumed she had contraception under control. Did she forget to take a pill? And he doesn't ask the question streaking back and forth in his head like a panicked bird trapped inside a house. *Is she going to keep it?*

He dawdles over his stroganoff while she finishes her salad. Then she signals Missy for the check and smiles at him.

"Tonight's on me."

Since the first night, he's always paid because he's the man. What does this mean? He feels like he's losing control. But he lets her pay. They walk wordlessly out of the restaurant. They stop beside her car and look at each other. He sees those little waves of desire in her eyes that will become big ones if he wants.

"Are you coming over?"

The lioness still leaps at his command, but tonight it's different. It's like returning to the scene of the crime. She puts her arms around his neck and pulls his face toward hers. He feels her pelvis rub against his as they kiss.

She unlocks the door, they enter, and she closes the door behind them. For the first time, he sees her tiny apartment as more than a love nest he visits two or three times a month. He examines her furniture and knick-knacks. What's a prized purchase, what's from charity? Is that Oriental vase something she inherited? He remembers her once mentioning a mother and a brother, and a dad that had disappeared after the divorce, and sure enough there are pictures on the table he never noticed before. Cathy has a real life she lives each day. This is the home of the mother of his child.

67

She takes his hand and leads him to the bedroom. She begins kissing him, and he kisses her back, no longer feeling like a man with two wives. He and Diana don't have children. They never really sealed the deal. Cathy stops kissing him, sensing he's distracted. She takes his face in her hands.

"I get it. I'm pregnant. If you want to run out that door and never come back, it's okay. No judgment."

She's going to keep it. How can she afford a child? She has some crap office job, better than minimum wage, but not much. She's never asked for money, even when the collection agency was after her. He looks in her eyes, sees those waves, bigger now, and feels the undertow of lust.

"I'm not going anywhere except to bed with you."

She lifts her shirt off over her head, pushes back her hair from her face, and reaches behind to undo her bra. It drops to the floor. They embrace, and slowly his kisses travel from her lips, down her neck, to her breasts. He circles her nipple with his tongue, feeling it rise, harden, and hears her breathing change. He imagines a baby at her breast in nine months, wonders how that's different than what he's doing. She undoes his pants. He steps out of them. As she drops to her knees and he watches her work on him, he compares her to Diana. Cathy is the clear winner. He pushes her back on the bed. Tonight he wants to be on top. After they finish, instead of dressing and leaving as he always has before he says, "I'm staying the night, if that's okay."

She looks at him, eyebrows raised. "What about Diana?"

He smiles. "What about her?"

Diana demanded he choose. Boy, is she going to be surprised.

In the morning, they make love again, and then, lying beside her on the sticky sheets, he tells her.

"I'm going to marry you."

"What?"

He's being rude. Technically, he has to ask.

"I mean, I want to marry you. Right away. I'll have my lawyer file divorce papers today. What do you say? Will you be my wife?" Of course, she'll say yes. She's a low-income mother-to-be in desperate need of a provider to take care of her. He's going to be her hero.

"Are you serious?"

"Serious as a heart attack." His mind spins with plans. He'll buy them a house in a neighbourhood with good schools. He'll put a sandbox and a wading pool in the back yard. She props up on her elbows and looks at him.

"What about the baby?"

"I want you to have it." If it's a boy, he'll insist they name it after him.

She sits up all the way. Her mouth is open, shaped in a big O, as if she's waiting for the right words to tumble out, but none do. She closes her mouth. Then she smiles. Her eyes are bright with surprise, as if she's just won the lottery.

"I'm sorry to act this way, it's just that I didn't see this coming. But yes, yes, I'll marry you!"

They hug. She squeezes him tight, then relaxes into a clinging that says she doesn't want to let go. Well, she doesn't have to. He holds her tenderly. He feels her body pulse. She's crying. He feels like a god.

While Cathy fixes breakfast, he texts his attorney. *Prepare divorce petition for me ASAP. You have our personal information from estate planning.* He notices numerous texts from Diana last night. Rather than respond, he pulls up email. What he has to say to Diana is too much to cram into a text.

He composes a measured but complete renunciation of his marriage. He's not assigning blame, he says, but were fault weighed, he could not say that Diana would fare well in the balance. He tells her he's "planted my flag on new land" and steps into the future with the sense he's finally discovered who he is. He urges her to do the same, tells her he wishes her all the best and that his attorney (formerly *their* attorney) will be forwarding papers for her to sign. He gives her permission to continue living in their house until it's sold or she buys him out. If she needs money, he can send some, but since she has a good job and he knows their monthly expenses "don't be too greedy about it." He attaches a photo of Cathy, referring to her as his "fiancée". *We're expecting a baby* he types, then deletes so everyone can pretend the child was conceived after he and Diana separated. He doesn't want to break Diana's spirit. He taps send.

He picks up his boxers from the floor, puts them on, and pads into the kitchen. Cathy is in her robe, spatula in hand, French toast in the skillet. Wanting to help, he opens the refrigerator and takes out a package of bacon. She shakes her head.

"I need to throw that away. No more bacon. Nitrates are bad for the baby."

He likes bacon, but she's right. He makes a show of dropping the package of bacon in the trash. She smiles.

"You'll be a wonderful husband."

"And father, too. Did you see me throw that nitrate-infested bacon away for the baby?"

She laughs. "I'm lucky. Most men don't want to marry into a package deal."

"Well, I'm not most men."

"I'll even put your name on the birth certificate if you want."

He laughs at her joke. But as he inserts a bite of French toast in his mouth, it hits him. He's not the father.

About the author
Mike Wilson's work has appeared in magazines including *The Pettigru Review, Fiction Southeast, Mud Season Review, The Saturday Evening Post, Deep South Magazine, Still: The Journal, Barely South Review,* and *Anthology of Appalachian Writers* Vol. X. He's author of *Arranging Deck Chairs on the Titanic.* He resides in Lexington, Kentucky, USA.

Impossible Promise

Barrington Gordon

I stood, taking in the exterior of St. Bevan's Hospital. Its grey, brutalist concrete structure looked forlorn, staring back at me. Its compound eyes cried as nature coated its face with ample, line-pouring rain. This had become part of my daily routine. I laughed at the word "routine." Somewhere in my psyche, it implied "normality," but there was nothing normal about watching my son David being eaten away by what I was told several weeks ago.

Here I am again. Armed with the obligatory gift of fruits: tangerines, grapes, and bananas. Well, that's what I was brought up to do by my parents, and I saw them practise. When visiting *the sick*, bring fruit. The blue carrier bag hammered against my thigh, wind-driven protesting, telling me to move from the spot, but try as I may, my leaden legs refused to budge. A car horn jolted me out of my reverie. I hadn't realised I was standing on the last stretch of the driveway leading up to the hospital. A gust of wind sent winter leaves sailing into the air like swallows reaching for the sky on their winter jaunt to warmer climates.

Visions of David came back to me. My son's small frame; his spidery looking limbs silhouetted in the mid-day sun as he sprinted away from me. He ran with gusto towards the Caribbean coral-coloured sea. The innocence of his delightful laughter warmed me with pure, unadulterated pleasure. Would that be our last holiday together? Unbeknownst to me, the bad news hung on the horizon, six months away – too far for the human eye to see. The "not so good news" as the doctor put it, I clearly saw now, was shrouded by clouds, of parental pride hidden in time by clear blue skies. The ignorance of human foresight to comprehend what was coming had scuppered me.

I stared at my son, a beautiful mocha-coloured child. He lay entrapped in a maze of paraphernalia. A spider's web of medical cables and gizmos surrounded him, seemingly holding David hostage. I wanted to free him, but there was nothing I could do; these were for his good. So I ritualistically replaced the fruit that once again had not been eaten. *Normal?* There was nothing *normal* about him having breast cancer – let alone a rare form of it.

"Breast cancer!" My ears refused to take in the bombshell the doctor had just delivered. "Surely that was what women normally get! Sorry... I mean, well, I don't know what I mean or think," I bumbled replying to the news, trying to find words not invented yet by human language, desperately trying to make sense of David's test results. "No one should have breast cancer – any fucking cancer!" That my young son should contract it was beyond belief. I looked at the pubescent intern as he delivered the news.

"An 'Aberration,' he called it. *Aberration?* The word drummed in my ear like the description of some alien parasite.

"But how?" I'd asked. There was some guarded explanation of this. Our family's DNA. Confused, I asked which parent it might have come from. The doctor, who looked like a sixth-former – a mere child himself – seemed thrown by my questions. His fingers combed through his mop of ginger hair resting nervously on his desk; spider-like, they thumbed away, unsure where else to go, as if seeking refuge. No route of escape is found. I'm not sure what I heard or even understood after the news was delivered; its bolt of lightning tore through my mind, burning white hot.

"Your wife or partner...." His gaze wandered

uncomfortably to my hand. I looked down. The fist clenched and unclenched. My nails had cut into my palm. Crimson blood seeped out of it. The doctor's left eye twitched; nerves were getting the better of him. He went to continue, but I cut him off.

"There's no one else, David, my son was adopted." My tongue felt like weighted cotton wool in my mouth. Once again, the teenage-looking physician appeared stumped. Then he started up again and spoke. My mind faded him out, and his voice became a white noise. I needed silence to think and process the tsunami of information. I tried to hear what he was saying. I know I saw his lips move but heard very little. I wanted, no, needed, for him to shut up. My eyes wondered at the various medical certificates and qualifications on his office wall. He looked so small and skinny – no more than five feet five.

"Chemotherapy, radiotherapy, medication, *switch off his machine*." These last words crashed me back into reality. At what point I'd launched at him, hands around his neck, and security guards hauling me off him, I don't know. I remembered his breath smelling of coffee, or was it cigarettes? The embarrassment and shame that washed over me after this hung in my soul like the stench of rotting meat on a hot summer day. This wasn't me – not like me. It was a sensation that I couldn't even explain to my doctor.

Back in my son's hospital room, I breathed as I tried to slow my heart rate and calm myself, stemming the creeping feeling of panic threatening to engulf me. Such feelings had become more frequent, as had my visits. I was there every day and was familiar with most of the staff on his wing. I promised not to cry today, but that had also become part of my daily ritual. *Promise*. The word echoed in my mind. When David was younger, I'd also made him a promise, one that now haunts me.

I'll always protect you and make sure nothing or no one harms you.

It was a ridiculous promise, one I now hate, causing me to despise myself. How could I have made that impossible promise? All I had to do was provide food, love clothing, and happy times. What made me think that giving up my job and working from home would be enough? What made me think that reading bedtime stories and visits to *our* favourite bookshop would be enough? What made me think that loving him with all my heart and soul would be enough? What an immature fool I'd been. I sat at his bedside, lost in thought. Questions scurried around like ants invading my mind; none of them could be answered.

The glass I'd been holding dropped from my hand, shattered, and startled me awake. Sleep was like a long-lost lover; it teased and evaded me when I expected it. Seven-year-old David lay there. His small, skinny chest rose and fell. I counted the ribs over and over. He seemed so peaceful. Tubes came out of his body from all directions; his small face seemed dwarfed, engulfed by the transparent mask now helping him. The breathing machine kept his heart pumping, lessening the strain. It reminded me of an accordion expanding and contacting rhythmically. A monitor on the right side of his bed measured his vitals and motored away. A hermetically sealed pod surrounded his bed with an air purifier. This was his *bubble* tent, as nurses christened it. It was like watching a sci-fi movie about people being cryogenically frozen. Strangely, David loved it – that sci-fi feel, it's his favourite genre.

Bells and buzzers whispered in the background; the orchestra of medical equipment kept him alive. I sat there, contained, suited up like an astronaut. The biohazard-looking gear was essential for keeping his environment clinically clean. Preventing any possibility of further infecting or compromising his immune system was crucial. I played along with his little game – a space adventure. David loved our "space suits", as he christened them. Nurses came in periodically, pressed buttons, and made him *comfortable*. His bedding was changed regularly, along with air filters, drips, and other stuff. It was a maze of mind-boggling alchemy. Among all this confusion lay a most beautiful being, David, my son.

"Hello, spaceman!" I stirred from a restless sleep, looked up, and realised David must have been watching me all this time. I'd dozed again. A smile broke out on my face. He beamed back one. My world lit up, and I felt light-headed.

"Hi, Son. How are you feeling today?" He frowned. I played along and addressed him with his proper title. "I mean... Commander!" I mimicked a salute. He reciprocated.

"A little tired, Captain." His voice was muffled by his mask. I strained to hear. "I've been exploring Mars today.... I have good news. I've located the signal. There is *life* here." My heart jumped at the word. He sought it in his imaginary world, but in this reality, he was... I couldn't allow myself to entertain the *D* word – the possibility of it – as he now lay there in palliative care. I think the space game was also his way of coping with not being mobile. Space, his bedroom, was covered with stars and planetary systems. He didn't know I now slept in it. This was the only way I got some sleep now and again. Besides his picture at night, the Buzz Light-year toy was the last face I saw. "Infinity and beyond!" David shouted and then started coughing and spluttering. He must have noticed the concern etched across my face.

"You know, the doctor said you're not supposed to do things like that," I reminded him. The edge in my voice wasn't meant to sound harsh. He cringed.

"You mean the spaceship's doctor," he asserted.

"Correction, sir, the spaceship doctor." It was the language we now cultivated; everything now had to have some sort of reference to science fiction or space. Nothing else was allowed. That was our deal.

"Captain?" David spoke. "You said you had something to talk to me about? Going into Cryo—" I could see he was struggling with the term.

"Cryogenic sleep, Commander." I jumped in and helped him finish it reluctantly. My heart plummeted. I recalled Dr Jeffers raising the issue that the strain of all the drugs and treatments were eroding his immune system. Too many complications were occurring. To control them, his best chance was a procedure that would involve inducing him into a co— *But*, why did there always have to be a "but"?

"We need to put him in a controlled sleep." I looked at him angrily. "But it is risky…" I interrupted him.

"You mean a… coma."

The doctor continued. "He might…"

My mind blocked out the memory of the doctor's voice. I'd looked at him hating him even more. I hated everyone these days. Nothing said could console me. I could feel him looking at me carefully, assessing my reaction to this news, especially after I tried to strangle, no, attacked him. He seemed jittery and nervous. A nurse was with him. I wondered if this was more of a precaution for his protection since *the incident*, as my doctor referred to it. The police said no charges would be brought, thankfully.

The doctor continued, his young face seeming to grow older as he spoke. His fingers combed through that mop of ginger hair once more as he fixed me with a stare heavily emphasising his words. "…otherwise," he continued, "…he could plummet into an uncontrolled one where the outcome…"

His brow furrowed. I could see the cogs of his mind grinding as he fought to find suitable words, "…be… a less," he paused, searching. "…might not be so favourable." Immediately, my mind fell into a starless abyss, fighting over how I was going to explain this to David. How do I tell him? How could I hide, giving away the fact that I might lose him? Then it came to me.

"David, Commander," I stuttered, swallowing hard. "We need to send you on a *special* mission. He looked excited. I felt sad. "We need to send you to the north side of Mars." My body was tensing; *relax*, I told myself. "This is a new directive from Space Command. The signs of life you detected, we need to make first contact."

"Is that to do with the bacon we sent out?" We burst out laughing. I think we both had visions of…

Then he interrupted, vocalising it. "Funny that… Imagine us crashing into pieces of bacon in space, huh?" More laughter, then he gasped. "Beacon!" His laughter rapidly changed into body-wracking coughs and spluttering again. "I wonder if I've picked up some alien infection." I hugged him carefully, weaving my hands and arms through the spider's web.

"Captain!" he gasped. "You know you shouldn't hug me." Somewhere, deep down, I lied to myself. The hug was just as much for me as it was for him.

"It's OK, Commander. The ship's doctor said I could as long as I had my space suit on." I looked at him and wanted to tear it off, along with all the cables separating us from skin-to-skin human contact.

"Captain! Are you crying again?"

"No, it's just my suit steaming up, sir! The circulator filters. Engineering needs to repair them once more. Remember that's how we found them, sir? Micro organisms in the filters? That was how we suspected alien life forms existed." He played along with my story.

"Those Martians, can't trust anything. Say vigilant!" he scolded. Mischievously, he pretended to laugh again. I got scared, but realised he was joking.

"Commander, there is something else I need to share with you." I looked about suspiciously exaggerating my movements, like someone might be in earshot of our conversation. "This is top secret." David's chocolate-brown eyes expanded even more, and sadly, the sun shone off his hairless scalp; a gut-wrenching reminder of his condition.

"What is it, Dad... I mean, Captain," he corrected, quickly deepening his voice. He sounded even more senior. My eyes wondered around his room for a moment, jarring my emotions and settling on the wall of *get-well-soon* cards. All were handcrafted by school pupils and teachers alike and had something to do with space on them. At only five, David had firmly told me he wanted to be an astronaut. It seemed like just yesterday. Now, just two years later, here we were, living his dream, but with a piece of me dying daily.

"We will have to put you in Cryo to get you safely through their portal."

"You mean like a coma?" I froze. Where had he learned that term from? Ice shot through my veins, and I felt my resolve crumble. Had he noticed the change in my demeanour? Quickly, I continued forcing my mind not to entertain the thought that he may not return. A feeling of betrayal ate away at me for not telling him the real risks involved. Most of the time, he was in pain, but he tried to hide it from me. He was so incredibly brave. His courage made me feel inadequate. I just wanted it all to stop! I'd promised to protect him from pain, suffering, and everything else. Twice, he'd caught pneumonia. He was full of antibiotics and steroids. Other organs in his body were also broken down by the medication he was having to take. I don't think the hospital knew what to do, but I suspected they didn't know how to tell me this either; I could sense it. No parent should ever have to… His question interrupted my thoughts.

"What do you think, Captain?" he asked.

"It might be our best chance, Commander. First contact and all that." His eyes lit up again Guilt shredded my insides. Something flickered across his face. Doubt? My breathing hitched. He wondered for a while. Noises from machines filtered through my thinking, suddenly becoming unbearably loud, and then he saluted me. I breathed.

"I concur." The cacophony receded into the crevasses of my mind, morphing into its previous humdrum. "It's our best chance," he repeated authoritatively.

"Yes, Commander." He looked up at me.

"I'll take on the mission," he said proudly. A brief glow returned to his cheeks. He seemed happy again. I saluted him back.

"Yes, Sir."

Time with David always flew by. Maybe it was the pressure; hanging over me, that created this illusion. The doctor hovered in the wings like a hawk, ready to execute its prey, waiting for me to give the go-ahead. The countdown has begun. Only seven days remained to make up my mind. *Mission critical*, one of David's favourite phrases, echoed in my consciousness. When had it gone dark outside? One day less.

"Look, Captain!" I followed where his finger pointed. "The north star!" I smiled, and my space suit misted up again. I watched him fall asleep and made my weary way quietly out of the room. Each step felt like I was treading through quicksand on the moon. The gravity of the situation weighed me down. As I left the hospital, I bumped into Dr Jeffers. We were alone in a corridor. As the distance closed between us, he looked around, petrified, like a rabbit wanting to escape. I thought I'd put him out of his misery and save him the pain of asking me the question, especially being alone in my company.

"I've spoken with David." He looked at me, stunned. Or was it suspicion I detected, buried behind those eyes? "It's OK to go ahead with the… Cryo." He looked at me puzzled, and then realisation broke the surface of a smile. "I… I mean, induced…" I choked, not being able to finish the words.

"It's OK, Mr Adams." His voice dropped to barely a whisper. "I think David knows more than he's letting on." I looked up knowingly, but he'd already anticipated my question. "He asks the nurses a lot of intelligent questions. He also tells them he's worried… about leaving Captain Adams behind." My legs felt like they'd abandon me. I held on to the support rail running the length of the hospital's corridor.

How I made it home that evening was a blur. We'd agreed; there was no point in delaying. The procedure was to be performed tomorrow. I couldn't sleep all night. I sat in David's bedroom, reading all his space books, including the cards sent home for him, and just cried. I smelled his quilt, lavender mixed with mint. It was adorned with undiscovered worlds, which he loved telling stories about so much. I sobbed into its cover remorsefully. The next morning, I arrived at the hospital early. I entered the room, space-suited up.

"Morning, Son."

"Captain? Commander!" he righted." He saluted me.

"Commander!" I reciprocated, but I was unprepared for the sight before me. The room full of medical personnel. Like bees, they darted about conducting last-minute checks and preparations in *spacesuits*. I thought I recognised some. It was hard to tell; all were shrouded behind masks. Eyes flitted across me, avoiding contact. A fist welled up in my throat. I'd wanted these *last* moments to be private.

"Could you go through the final checks before the countdown with Mission Control Captain?" David's words grounded me back into reality. I could feel my whole body begin to vibrate with uncontrolled breathing. *Stay composed*, I berated myself.

"Yes, Sir!" I turned and closed my eyes. My suit was misting up. I pretended to speak into an intercom. "Repeat, please, ground control!" I paused a moment longer, breathing deeply. Eventually, I felt calm enough to speak. "All checks are confirmed! It's a go?" I spun back around and nodded at the staff present. "It's a go, team!" I announced. I took David's hand in mine. The protective gear separating us felt so invasive. I wanted to kiss Commander Adams, wish him well on his journey but couldn't. A nurse came forward and inserted a syringe into his drip.

"Commander. This will relax your muscles for the Cryo," she played along. His small mouth was full of so many happy teeth that it looked ridiculous.

"Godspeed, Sir!" I saluted. My body felt like it would snap with the rigidity with which I'd hailed him. David's eyelids fluttered slightly. The nurse nodded at me. I stepped forward and began the countdown. "Ten…" I heard him counting with me.

"Ten!" The excitement in his voice was palpable. He looked relaxed.

"Nine."

"Nine," he echoed. "All systems good." The voice of a child unknowingly calms his father.

"Eight." Instinctively, my hand travelled to my face, trying to brush a tear away. *Stupid!* I shouted inside my head.

"Eight." He smiled. His voice sounded distant. "All checks here are still good ground control."

"Seven." His fingers throbbed, clenching mine for a split second.

"Seven." A pinging sound travelled through the air. All eyes were averted to his monitor. The nurse pressed a button, scrutinising the device methodically. My heart somersaulted. She nodded at the doctor. His shoulders seemed to decompress, and mine followed.

"All good here, ground control," the nurse's muffled voice reassuringly chimed in. The blip on the monitor resumed its previous monotonous pulse range.

"Six." My voice sounded hoarse. *Hold it together, Captain*, I whispered.

"Six." David's eyes fluttered closed. I squeezed his hand a little firmer. I didn't want to look up. I felt like all eyes were on me.

"Five." I breathed deeply. Fire entered my lungs.

"Five." His hand was barely holding on to mine now.

"Four." A drunken smile slowly emerged on his lips.

"Four." His hand went limp. "Love… Dad."

"Three. His breathing surprisingly dropped to a raspy, deep snore. Nothing came back from his side.

"Three," a nurse uttered nervously.

"Tw—" I couldn't finish the countdown.

"Two." A glimmer of an adult voice took up the count.

"One." He's under someone's voice, uttered from far away.

Just before they took David to the theatre, I swear I heard him whisper something strange.

Dad? Let me go… You'll be all right. It sounded like a distant voice carried by the wind. Frantically, I looked around, but no one reacted. Was I hearing things? I needed to be sure.

"Is he supposed to be able to speak?" The medical team looked at me warily. My nerves felt fraught. Gently, Dr Jeffers placed a hand on my arm and guided me aside. Desperately, I craned my neck like a meerkat, trying to watch what the nurse was doing over his shoulder. He deliberately blocked my view. A ridiculous dance unfolded; avoidance steps from side to side. She scanned his vitals again via the portable black plastic monitor perched like a crow on the bar above his bed. I fought a losing battle to subdue the threatening panic, which was swelling like a tidal wave in my gut. Any second now, the dam of emotions would burst, sucking me under. "Did you hear that?" I shouted insistently. My eyes burrowed into his, demanding an answer.

"He's definitely *under* doctor," the nurse's harried voice confirmed. Her eyes embarrassingly scanned me, quickly moving on to her other duties.

"Mr Adams." The doctor spoke, moving slightly to his left, blocking my view, determined to regain my attention. "Leave it to the ground crew." Behind his mask, a smile hollowed out where his mouth would be, air sucking in his P.P.E. His eyes glimmered reassuringly. "He's on his mission; now allow us to do ours… Captain?" Him uttering the rank bestowed by David drained all the fight out of me. Instantly, I felt my shoulders wilt. Helplessness concreted me into the spot. I watched the other staff wheel my son away to the operating room. Dr Jeffers delayed his parting. His hand came up, resting on my left shoulder. He stared into my eyes. "Why don't you wait in the family room?" I saw his eyes flicker, and then he said, "The Mission Control Centre, Captain." The charade resumed. "You can almost see it from here; follow this corridor," he said, pointing a blue latex gloved finger. "Turn left. Doors immediately in front of you. OK?" A last tap on my arm, and he was gone.

I staggered to a wheelchair stranded outside David's room, pondering my son's words. *Dad? Let me go… You'll be all right.* Did he know what was really happening to him? Distant sounds from surrounding wards filtered through my hearing. They pulsed throughout the hospital's hallways, playing individual mechanical orchestral sounds in the background. An incessant coded musical language rose and fell. Reluctantly, I drifted off into a restless sleep.

Panic stricken I jolted awake. Quickly, my eyes refocused, taking in the time on my watch. An hour had lapsed! The familiar eyes of the nurse appeared in front of me. I must have fallen asleep.

"Why don't you go home and get some proper rest?" her voice soothed. Her eyes assessed my demeanour. "You *must* be exhausted."

I'd been dreaming that we'd been piloting our spaceship, I was trying to land us on the far side of Mars, the Promethei Terra; it's bearing 58°0'0"S, 60°0'0"E. David looked elated in the dream. Now, awakened, her smile reminded me of his. Nurse Ashley's plump, cherry-cheeked white face looked so assuring. I wondered if I was still dreaming. I stretched, pushing the sleep at bay. "I have to do some rounds now, but I'll be back within the hour," she said, smiling. "You'd better not be here when I return," she wagged a playful finger at me. "We'll call you soon as he is out… rest, for him," she pleaded.

I saw shadows moving about. As my eyes adjusted, the space morphed into familiar surroundings – our second home, David's hospital room. Nurse Ashley was unzipping herself out of the hermetically sealed tent and about to leave.

"Ahm!" I swallowed, trying to lubricate my throat. I'd slept with my mouth open again. I'd startled her; a hand fluttered over her chest. "Sorry."

"Oh no. I woke you," she said, sounding apologetic. I nodded *no*. "You were knocked out, so I wheeled you in. We thought it best to leave you to rest. You're obviously, exhausted.

"How is he?" My voice sounded rusty. My throat felt like I'd drunk a pint of sand. I rubbed my eyes, forcing the last remnants of sleep from them

"He's stable, asleep." I felt her eyes follow me as I got up and went to look at him. Shortly, she stood beside me. "The doctor will be along in a moment to speak with you." Her head tilted forward, taking me in. "Would you like a cup of tea?" Yes, I nodded nonchalantly. My eyes closed momentarily. I was still having trouble staying awake. The spider's web of cables around David had increased noticeably. She rubbed my arm, sensing something. "You may as well rest now, my lovely." My eyes fluttered. I heard a click as the door closed. She'd left the room. David looked so defenceless against it all. I kissed my fingers and touched his tent. I swayed, nearly lost my balance, and held on to a side table. Final warning: I went to sit back down.

The spaceship was listing, and we were losing control. Crashing was inevitable. Bells, buzzers, and alarms squawked from everywhere. My eyes flew open. I jumped up out of my seat and back into reality. David was convulsing. I rushed to his side, unzipped the tent, and held him. His eyes screwed tight as his small body contorted. A guttural scream filled the room. "Pain!" he cried. Tears ran down his cheeks. Suddenly, the seizure stopped as quickly as it had started. I stood back, staring down at him. Then, as clear as day, he looked me straight in the eyes and spoke.

"You have to let me go, Dad."

Fearful, I looked at all the flashing symbols in desperation. Why was no one here?

"It's all right," he whispered.

I pressed the emergency red buzzer repeatedly. He looked at me like he was sorry for me and nodded, *no*. I hung my head and bawled. I prayed for that door to burst open. I couldn't lose him. "It's OK, Dad." I looked around, not knowing what to do. I willed the medical team to be here now! "Seal the spacecraft, Dad." He stared at the wardroom door.

"What!" slavered out of my mouth awkwardly.

"It's time. Dad... it hurts." His voice hit home as his body arched violently again. His eyes rolled to the back of his head. His teeth ground horribly. "Ahh!" he screamed. I stroked his forehead, trying to calm him. His chest pounded up and down.

"Can't let you go, Son." I was crying and dribbling at the same time. Suddenly, he was lucid again. His next words made up my mind.

"Hurts... too much... Go on... O-Kay," he stuttered. Please!" he begged. "Seal the hatch." Before I knew what was happening, my feet had already carried me to the door. My hand came up, shaking, and locked it. "Hold me tight, Dad... I'm going to land." I rushed back to him. Our bodies shook as I tried to comfort him. Now I understood what he was going through. He sobbed into my breast as the pain reached a crescendo. I tore my protective suit off and held him. In seconds, I was soaked. Sweat poured from him into my chest. The noise of medical personnel banging on the door mingled distantly with the sounds of the spaceship engines. We were going to make contact with the far side of Mars. It was deafening. My eardrums felt like they'd burst. "We're here. Reached," drifted into my ear. His breathing shallowed then, spaced further and further apart. His body fell limp. He smiled his drunken baby smile, and then he was gone.

I kissed, hugged, and rocked my son. Through his pyjamas covered with planets, I felt every rib. His feather-light body looked like a china doll at peace. Maybe I had achieved the impossible promise. His pain and suffering had come to an end.

About the author

Barrington Gordon's short story entitled "The Chair" has been published in *Voice Memory Ashes Lest we Forget*, and "Grandfather's Feet" in *Whispers in the Walls*, a Birmingham anthology, endorsed by Bonnie Greer and Benjamin Zephaniah. BBC Radio 4 featured this as part of its short story profiling. In 2024 he has been published in the anthology *Bilston Banquet, A feast of words* by Bilston Writiers.

Barrington has worked across communities in the Midlands for several decades. His writing goal encapsulates uplifting people who, in reality, just need a little support like we all do to feel and be human. Civic Leicester published his last poem "Black & White TV-Sound Bites" in *Welcome to Britain*.

Janet, More than a Friend

Lynne English

Janet is a dog. When I talk about Janet everyone thinks I am talking about a person but she is the cutest King Charles Spaniel you could ever wish to meet and I love her. I love her more than my ex-husband and that's understandable. I am better off without him in my life. And I love her almost as much as Simon and Susie, my son and daughter who have both moved away, and hardly bother with me at all.

I'm quite a lonely person really and Janet is my best buddy. I talk to her when we're at home on our own and sometimes she will sit quietly with her head tilted to one side as if she is listening to me intently. What she is really thinking is, "Where is my dinner?" I go against everyone who told me not to do it, because I let Janet sleep on my bed, and sometimes if I've nodded off in the armchair at night, she will gently nudge my leg to waken me, as if to say, "Come on, Mum, time for bed", and together we will climb the wooden hill to bed and settle down, side by side.

I used to have a busy life, bringing up the children as a single parent, whilst combining working part-time as a secretary in a health centre, only a few hours a week when the kids were little, and then full-time when they were at senior school. It wasn't easy and although I'm obviously glad Covid wasn't around in the nineties. It would have been my dream to work from home. It's ironic really, but that's life and things are meant to be I suppose. I had to take early retirement from work at the age of fifty-two as I developed rheumatoid arthritis and the swelling on my hands was so bad that my fingers were gnarled and bent. Simon used to say they looked like witches' hands. Typing became so painful and that was the only thing I was good at so I had no

89

option really other than to take early retirement. Susie had made a new life for herself in Birmingham with her friend Sally and travelled a lot so I hardly saw her. Simon lived locally for a while then decided to move to Kent to be nearer his dad. I was sad about that because his dad wasn't in the picture when Simon and Susie were growing up but then he became the Fabulous Father and bounced back into their lives, just like a bad penny. Susie was having none of it but Simon lapped it up, or possibly milked it, I'm not sure, but either way he moved to Kent and his dad gave him some money for a deposit on a flat. I would never be able to afford to do that on my meagre NHS pension and PIP allowances, so there I was, home alone. But not for long.

On a whim I went to the local Animal Shelter one rainy Sunday afternoon, I was so bored at home. A litter of puppies, King Charles Spaniels, had just been brought in; apparently the mum had died shortly after four of them had been born as complications had set in as she was trying to deliver the fifth puppy and sadly they both died. The puppies needed to be hand reared and the owners couldn't cope which is why they were brought in to the Animal Shelter.

I'm not normally one who makes spontaneous decisions, I usually procrastinate for ages before making big changes but on that Sunday I made my mind up – I wanted a puppy! I hurried to see the nice assistant and I was glad I was wearing gloves because he wouldn't be able to see the state of my fingers, he might worry I wouldn't be able to manage to hold the lead or look after a dog properly. But it was all quite straightforward really. I was allowed to choose which puppy I wanted as I was the first to see them so I chose the one who bounded over to see me, she was just the cutest puppy ever. I decided to call her Janet after my mum and she looked like a Janet, the curly fur on her little head looked like the perm my mum once had, back in the sixties. I wasn't allowed to take her home for another seven weeks but I went every Sunday to see her and have a cuddle. In those interim weeks I got prepared – checked the garden to make sure it was safe, bought a stair gate because I thought Janet might decide to try out the stairs, and went crazy buying toys and a luxury bed. I splashed out on a pen but it was only ever used as a hiding place for Janet's "treasures" that she would go and check on throughout each day. The day I brought Janet home from the Shelter was one of the happiest days of my life.

Janet was the making of me, she bounded into my life with zest and vigour and she gave it to me. I can't say she put a spring in my step because my arthritis often gave me such pain in my knees and ankles that I had trouble walking, I could never have skipped along. I was happy; Janet made me happy. I rang Simon and Susie to tell them the good news and they were really pleased for me. Susie even rushed up to meet Janet the weekend after she came home.

Janet was my buddy and we made each other happy, she knew she was loved, she had walks, lovely food and a warm bed and cuddles at night. I had unconditional love, a waggy tail to greet me whenever I came into a room, and good company. Janet sensed when I was in pain and would walk sedately by my side when we were out instead of haring off when she spotted a squirrel in the park. We quickly got in a routine and sadly this is when it started to go wrong.

My arthritis didn't improve even when the Specialist put me on strong injections and much as I loved taking Janet out for a walk, I did struggle sometimes with the pain in my knees. We were creatures of habit, Janet and I; we would go out for a walk at about 10am every day, come rain or shine, taking the same route to the park. Sometimes we would meet people and Janet would love having a little "play date" for a few minutes. I actually enjoyed this, chatting to people, before I got Janet I would have avoided such situations and not gone anywhere. One day we were coming back from the park when I realised we were being followed by a man. My knees were really painful that day and it was raining so we were quite literally trudging along. I tried to hurry home but couldn't. Eventually we made it to the back door and by this time I was getting nervous as I could hear the clomping of boots behind me. I fumbled with the keys, managed to open the door and then dropped the keys. Janet sat patiently by my side whilst I scrabbled for them.

I pulled Janet into the kitchen and tried to shut the door behind us but I was pushed backwards inside. Janet stopped in her tracks, puzzled. She was actually a pretty useless guard dog because she loved and trusted everyone, she thought everyone wanted to be her friend. She sat there expectantly as the man closed the door behind us, slamming it shut and turning the deadlock. I started panicking and could feel myself sweating and my hands were shaking. I just didn't know what to do, I was literally standing there wringing my hands, like they do in the movies when things go wrong. The man told me to sit down, then sneeringly told me he had been watching me for weeks, told me I must lead a very boring life as I was so predictable. He told me I was an easy target as I walked like a cripple. He laughed. Janet moved closer to me, her tail not wagging any more, still puzzled. The man moved as if he was going to kick Janet away from me. I jumped up and found the courage to tell him to leave the dog alone. "What do you want?" I pleaded, "I've got some money but nothing really valuable. Take what you want and then leave us alone, please."

The man laughed. By now I was really scared. The man was tall and stocky; he would soon overpower me, and Janet, who now sensed something was wrong and started to whimper. Almost in slow motion the man walked towards

Janet and this time he did kick her. He booted her so hard that her paws left the ground and she fell backwards. I hurried towards her, but my right knee gave way and I wasn't quick enough to reach Janet. I stumbled and fell forward as the man kicked Janet again, who yelped in pain. "Please leave Janet alone!" I cried plaintively, "Take whatever you want but please don't hurt my dog!"

Janet was quivering, clearly terrified. The man picked her up and Janet started barking. He carried her towards the bedroom, threw her in and slammed the door shut behind him. I could hear Janet barking frantically for about five minutes, heard her scrabbling at the door, then it all went quiet. With horror it dawned on me that the small window in the bedroom was open and Janet had probably jumped up on the bed, gone across the bedroom table, and escaped.

I pleaded to the man to just take what he wanted and go. He laughed again, so much I could see spittle. He was repulsive. I was a gibbering wreck, pathetic really, but so shocked and scared I didn't know what to do. The man's mobile phone rang. He answered it, speaking in monosyllables, eventually terminating the call, saying, "Just five minutes." He opened a holdall and then started rummaging around in my bureau, grabbing my cheque book, driving licence, passport and a tin where I was saving £1 coins. He then asked me where my handbag was and took my purse and wallet of credit cards. I just sat there stunned, worrying about Janet. After a few minutes I heard a screech of brakes and saw a brown van pull to a halt outside the lounge. The man ran to the door, I guessed it was the getaway van, and then he stopped when he heard someone screaming outside. He turned and ran out the back door.

I thought my heart had stopped, I was paralysed with fear, and then I jumped into action and hurried outside. The driver of the van had run off and I saw, to my horror, my darling

Janet lying in the road, covered with a coat and a lady standing over her, crying. I hurried to Janet and scooped her up, there wasn't actually much blood but I knew straightaway that she was gone. I stood there motionless for what seemed an eternity, holding my best friend in my arms, just looking at her. Other people came over to see what was going on and then the police arrived.

This all happened five months ago. The lady who was first on the scene when Janet was hit had managed to take a photo of the van and the police had tracked down the driver, and eventually the thief, and both were arrested. I didn't go to Court, there was no point, but I heard that they were given prison sentences. I didn't care. I don't care about anything. My dear sweet Janet is no longer here; what is the point of caring? Simon and Susie's lives go on as usual, everyone's lives go on as normal, even the evil men who robbed me and killed Janet will eventually go back to their old lives. But not me.

Janet put the light back in my life, now I am in darkness. There is no good news for me; I am just so so sad. I won't be here much longer. Writing this is cathartic for me, I have told my story, I have made my will, leaving a large chunk of money to the Animal Shelter, this will be good news for them. How I miss Janet.

About the author
Lynne English is an Essex writer of short stories and poetry.

Lynne has an honest and open style of writing, enjoying, at times, the darker side of humour. She explores the quirks and nuances of being human, drawing carefully on an expanse of knowledge gathered during a lengthy career working for the NHS and the Bank of England.

Lynne invites the reader to really question the mundane and ordinary with humour and ease.

When not writing or managing a large team of clinicians and other staff at work, she enjoys spending time with family and friends, finding treasures in charity shops and watching *Killing Eve*!

Mistaken Identity

Liz Cox

I received the news on a Saturday. I know it was a Saturday because Simone was home from school, and we had intended to go shopping. She was disappointed, you know what teenagers are like, but she didn't ask why our plans had been changed. She did look at me a little bit funny though and then flounced out.

I remember sitting on the sofa, gripping the letter between both hands, and staring. I recall picking up the buff envelope (good news never comes in a buff envelope) from the doormat and turning it over. There it was, in bold type, black ink staring back at me. Mrs Joanne Feather. I didn't know this person, then I remembered. It was addressed to me. Why? I examined the postmark, tracing it with my forefinger as if feeling for a clue. It was franked Ministry of Defence. What did they want with me? I slid my finger under the flap, worked it open and removed the contents. The stiff cream paper crackled as I unfolded it. The kettle was whistling unheeded on the kitchen worktop.

Dear Mrs Feather...

There it was again, I didn't recognise this Mrs Feather; she had ceased to exist ten years ago. I could feel tears forming and wiped them away with the sleeve of my white jumper, leaving an irritating smudge of black.

Dear Mrs Feather,

We would like to inform you that we believe we have located the whereabouts of your husband Sergeant Thomas Feather. It was originally thought that he had been lost in action, but we have had news

which contradicts this. Please could you contact us on this number as soon as possible.
Yours sincerely,
General Sir Giles Easton.

I turned it over; nothing on the back. Had I read it correctly? They wanted me to contact them. Why? Was he alive? Should I be excited? I wasn't. A blackness descended. Simone was only three when he disappeared, and I would have given anything to have him home. I had lain awake night after night, staring at the dark void, wondering if he was somewhere out there in the universe. But that had passed and was redacted to a tiny corner in my mind, buried underneath more urgent things. But now? What had previously been contained, accepted, lived with, wept over, was resurrected into a possibly living, breathing reality that I didn't want to process. Our life is good, settled. I had married again when Simone was ten, my marriage to Tom dissolved. Colin was a good husband and a great stepdad to Simone. How would he feel? How would Simone feel? How did I feel? I tucked the letter behind the bread bin.

On Monday morning, after I had dropped Simone off at school, I made a coffee and retrieved the letter from its hiding place. Spreading the page out on the table amongst the toast crumbs and sticky patches of marmalade, I pressed it down firmly, then dialled the number. I re-read the letter while listening to the *brrr brrr brrr* at the other end. The paper was now stained with coffee and peppered with crumbs. I heard a dog barking in the street. Had the postman been? Just one more ring, I promised myself like a child playing games, and then I would hang up. It had to be some sort of scam. I was about to replace the receiver when I heard a woman's voice say, "Good morning, General Easton's office, how may I help you?"

She had to repeat herself, "How may I help you?"

"Hello... err – I'm Mrs Feather, or rather I was, I received a letter from your office on Saturday." The words came out in a rush, and I didn't even recognise my own voice.

"Good morning, Mrs Feather, if I could have the reference on the top of the letter and then I can put you through to the general."

The paper was shaking in my hands, so I scrunched the letter between my fingers to keep it still. Surely this had to be a mistake. I straightened the letter, peered at the top and read the number out to her. I took a swig of my now-cold coffee, gripped the table, and waited.

"Hello, Mrs Feather, I'll put you through now." There was a click, then another deeper voice was at the end of the line.

"Good morning, Mrs Feather, I'm General Easton." I raised my eyebrows. God! How many "good mornings" would I have to endure before we got to the point?

"Good morning, Sir." I waited not knowing if I should speak or wait to be spoken to. I was, for a split second, an army wife again.

"Well..." he seemed a little nervous, "we have received notification that a man meeting the description of your late husband has been found alive and well." He cleared his throat, "We need you to meet with us to confirm his identity. Can you come to the Ministry next week?"

"I'm not sure I can, Sir, I have a daughter to consider. She's got a dance competition coming up, and she's working towards exams. I would need to find someone to look after the dog... my husband is away working." I was aware that I was babbling on. Was Colin still my husband?

I slammed the phone down and stared into space. The telephone rang, I hesitated before picking it up. How could I make this go away?

"Mrs Feather," the voice was sharp, "we need to bring this matter to a conclusion. Are you not pleased to find out your husband may be alive?"

"Of course, Sir, it's fabulous news, but unexpected. It's a lot to take in." I raised my voice a couple of decibels trying to sound delighted. I didn't fool myself but didn't want the general to think I didn't care. To be honest, it was good news that he had possibly been found alive, but the implications flooded my mind. What would happen if it was him? Did I still love him? I took a deep breath. "I will make plans to come and see you next week. Please email the details; I don't think I can talk anymore." I could feel my voice breaking. After I gave him my email address, I replaced the receiver, and the tears began – loud racking sobs. The dog came and stood in front of me and put his paw on my knee. I stroked his soft ears then buried my face in his fur. "What shall I do, Charlie?" He licked my hand, no wiser than me. Should I let Simone know? Would she resent me if I didn't? Did she have a right to see her father – if it was her father – they had found? She didn't remember him. Colin knew the story when we married, but would he fear that I would leave him? Would our marriage be annulled? I couldn't bear that. If Tom had lived but been unable to return home, what kind of state was he in? Why didn't he come home? We still lived in the same house; he could have found us. After all the Ministry of Defence had found me. It felt like a physical blow in the pit of my stomach. Did he not want to come home? I bit my lip. Could he have another family? Did he even remember us? How could he disappear?

After I put the sugar in the fridge and re-washed the

clean washing instead of hanging it out, I knew I had to find out. I told Simone I had to go and see an old friend and would she be happy staying with her grandma for a couple of days and taking Charlie the dog with her. No problem there, she loved to be with Tom's mother. But I couldn't tell Grandma the truth. I wouldn't want to give her any false hope, so I told her the same story.

All the way to London on the train, I thought about Tom. I reflected on our flower-filled wedding in Cyprus on a balmy spring day, the strength and beauty of his lithe, tanned body, his raucous laugh and the way he ran his hands through his blond hair when irritated. I remembered the love in his deep blue eyes as he squeezed my hand when Simone was born. He doted on her, why would he not come home? I thought the unthinkable – were we living a lie? I shook my head to clear that insidious thought from taking root. Maybe he was badly injured and was suffering from memory loss. The letter had given no indication of this man's situation.

"Would you like coffee, madam? Are you OK, madam?"

"Yes, yes," managed to reply, as the stewardess' voice broke through. I knocked my handbag on the floor, spilling everything amongst the dirt and discarded food wrappings. She helped me to scoop everything back in and smiled. "I think you need a coffee," she said placing a cardboard cup on my table. I rubbed my cardigan sleeve on the dirty window to clean a space so I could watch the towns whizz by, but that was an effort too far. Closing my eyes, I let my thoughts run in time with the rhythm of the train, constant, incessant, unrelenting. I wiped my hands on my skirt, as if trying to rid myself of something unpleasant.

When I arrived at the Ministry, a soldier showed me to the general's office. It was very grand, no dirty windows here, just gold brocade curtains and a smell of lavender furniture polish. The wood gleamed as if judging me for my shortcomings. I sat in the outer office, hands and feet crossed, clutching my handbag between my fingers, whilst the secretary gave me a false professional smile.

I was duly ushered in by the same young soldier, all shiny buttons, and a straight back. As I entered, I saw people sitting around a very highly polished oak table, set neatly with crystal water glasses, a carafe in the centre. They all looked up. I felt the sweat on the palms of my hands. The man in the centre, presumably the general, stood up and extended his hand. I wiped my hand on the back of my skirt before accepting his.

"Good morning, Mrs Feather." There they went again more "Mrs Feather" and "Good Mornings", "Welcome to the Ministry."

I nodded; I couldn't speak, my tongue seemed too big for my mouth. I brushed my hair back from my eyes with my sweaty hand. Faces and colours merged into one, as the general made introductions. I couldn't tell you even now who was seated neatly around the table, but they all wore fancy gold braid and medals. I remember there being a large screen at the end of the room and me crying out because it was filled with a picture of Tom as I had known him, as I remembered him. From somewhere, I heard a disembodied voice saying, "Mrs Feather." I looked up.

"I'm not Mrs Feather, you've got the wrong person. I'm Mrs Ratcliffe." I remember the flash of irritation which creased the general's forehead. It was too much to take. Straightening my shoulders, I looked him right in the eye.

"Mrs Feather, please would you look at the folder on the desk in front of you." The voice was stern. In a trance, I opened the folder. "Is the man in the first photograph Tom Feather?" There in front of me was the same picture as on the screen but taken from a wider angle. It was an image of a man who looked like Tom, with a woman and a small girl and boy. I ran my fingers over the image. The flowers and trees were not English or even European. The woman was wearing a flamboyant red flower in her long black hair and was dressed in a brightly coloured sarong. It was Tom alright, and he looked happy. His smile was broad and his face and chest suntanned, obviously in perfect health. When was this taken? He was standing with one arm resting on the woman's shoulder and the other holding the hand of the little girl who had his smile – and that of Simone. It was my Tom.

"I'm not sure," I mumbled, focussing on my hands in my lap. "The man looks similar, but I don't think it's Sergeant Feather."

"We have reason to believe that this man *is* Sergeant Feather, and he went absent without leave whilst stationed in Malaya," the general insisted.

I shook my head. Low murmurs spread around the table like a Mexican wave; all eyes were fixed on me like searchlights. I leaned on the table leaving ghostly fingerprints in the polish and returned their gaze. I felt heat spreading up my neck.

"That man is not Tom." I slid the photo back into the folder and snapped it shut. My heart was beating wildly under my silk blouse, and I remember being surprised they could not see the delicate material fluttering.

"But you haven't looked at the other documentation yet." The general placed his hands on the table and leaned towards me. I backed away. "Please continue."

"I've seen enough, thank you. I need to leave now," I said rising from my chair, "that man is not Tom."

On the way home, I reflected on what I had done. I had lied to the government. Too bad. I was sorry that I couldn't show that picture to Tom's mother so she would have known he was alive, or to Simone. I would carry this secret to my grave. It would keep our family safe and also Tom's. This was the good news. But had I done the right thing? I would never know. I shook my head until I was dizzy to dislodge the guilt, but it wouldn't leave. I tightened my fingers around my coffee cup, until a little spilled over the top burning my hand. I could never forgive his betrayal, and would have to live everyday with the truth that he didn't want to come home.

About the author
Liz hails from North Yorkshire where she writes short stories and poetry. She is in the final stages of writing a novel. She enjoys all things medieval and has a PhD and MA in medieval literature. Her short stories have been published on line by *CaféLit* magazine and in various anthologies. Liz's first single author collection of short stories *Seen Through a Glass of Red* was published by Bridge House last year. At the time of writing, she is pleased that the snow has disappeared.

Ms Tidy

Keith Willson

I got through that first day somehow.

I woke up. Then I realised the head, the hangover. I stumbled into the living room and pulled the curtains. It was sunny. That split my head in half. Outside, the guy next door was washing his vibrant green Volvo to the sound of thumping Reggae, as usual. The thumping didn't help either.

It was just like any other Saturday – with a difference. I didn't want to start reconstructing the night before but I had to; we'd had the final row and Jill had left. A taxi at two in the morning to her sister's. She'd be back for her stuff. I knew I couldn't talk her out of it. When women say it's over they mean it. They don't come back no matter how much you try to change. This wasn't the first break up I'd had and I knew the rules by now. This time I wasn't going to waste the rest of my life on false hopes, however much it hurt.

A week passed and I felt like shit. I got through work. Didn't try to contact her, not that I knew where she'd gone, anyway. Eventually she called to say she'd arranged a van. The van came, I went out – she still had her key. When I got back it was on the hall table, just the key and no note. In the rooms there were dusty patches on the carpet, Rawlplugs hanging from the walls, where her shelves had been, and Blue Tak and torn wallpaper from her posters. That was it. She really had gone and I was desolate. But I'd started to write furiously.

"A writer is someone who WRITES!" she'd screamed during one of our rows, "not someone who *wants* to write or plays at writing!"

I thought that was unfair. I worked as hard at writing as anyone else. I just didn't get published. I had a job, she had a job. And in the evenings I wrote. I still do. Some of it was really good, even though I say so myself. Sometimes I would come down in the mornings and see what I'd written in the small hours and I almost imagined someone else had written it. After all the agonising and failure and shouting at myself I would eventually produce something I liked. But the publishers didn't. The manuscripts were returned with a scrawled note saying "Not quite for us" or with a standard rejection slip "The Editor has carefully read your work and although…" One even said "You need not submit further work to us."

Jill was scathing. "We both earn a fair wage. We could be out enjoying ourselves, but no. You just want to be a hero, have an excuse to beat yourself up. We never go out, we've got no friends."

"But," I argued, "I have lots of friends."

"I meant normal people," she said, "not a bunch of failed writers. You're the only one of them who actually writes anyway and it hasn't got you anywhere. The rest of them just discuss their food fads and their neuroses. That 'Workshop' you had. I could hear all of you from the garden. Listening to anyone in that group read was like being forced to watch someone slowly masturbate."

We would make up for a while. Then there was the premonition. "I *will* get published one day," I said to her.

"But I won't be there to see it," she said, sadly and suddenly. And a chill went through me. It took several weeks to get from there to the final row, but it came.

After she'd been for her things, I made up my mind to redecorate the flat. But I didn't get round to it. *It's far more important to write*, I told myself. I stayed up until three in the morning, getting up some days at seven for work. I could cope without much sleep – that was surprising. Maybe the rows and reconciliations had taken up more of the night than I thought anyway; I didn't suffer any more from long bouts of writing than I had done from long bouts of fighting.

A week after she'd picked up her stuff, two weeks after she'd left, it was late Sunday morning and there was someone at the door. *Her?*

A sly look through the curtains and I knew I didn't want to answer it. It was Derek. Derek was from the local Residents' Association. Nobody has dandruff nowadays, but you could imagine he did, even though the shiny shoulders of his navy-blue jacket were clean and his brown polyester trousers had been ironed once. His hair was too black, some unhealthy greasiness. He'd seen me and I couldn't escape. I opened the door.

"Raffle tickets?" he asked. He had an annoying voice. I've got nothing against accents but there are nice voices and horrible ones. "We're looking for funds to fence off some old railway land as a nature reserve."

Then he studied me more closely. "My God! You look awful, what's up? I'd better come in."

I made coffee.

"She was too good for you anyway," he said. "It seems the end of the world when it breaks up. When Ann finished with me I was going to kill myself. I got as far as the edge of the platform. I stood shaking like anything. Of course I couldn't do it – I came home and drank half a bottle of whisky. Took me weeks to get over it."

He looked around my front room, from the piles of paper on the table to the pile of washing on the floor and smirked. "Do what I did. What you need is a Mrs Tidy."

"I'm doing my best," I said, realising the state I'd let the flat get into, "but there's no motivation."

"I don't mean that," he said, looking more disreputable than ever. "I don't mean you need the place cleaned. I know exactly what you need. You need a woman to visit you once a week. Put a card in the shop window – Mrs Tidy wanted, three hours a week, time by mutual arrangement, to do hoovering, ironing etc. Something like that. She comes and does the work. You act like a gentleman for three weeks and then you subtly try it on. It works. We're all lonely, all need to feel wanted, all need to feel attractive. Don't harass them or anything like that. If they say no – apologise. Back off. Business as usual. Really sorry, misunderstood the signals, don't be offended etc. All the time you act like a gentleman, not a pervert. I've had three Mrs Tidys. It worked with all of them. Had two at the same time once. I had to mess up the place again after the first one, so the other one could tidy it.

"Derek," I said slowly, "that's just not politically correct. There's no way I'm doing that. All I want is Jill back again."

I had no idea what to do. Mr Majumdar in the shop gave me a card and a pen. "Write your advert. One pound fifty a week, two weeks in advance. It comes down after two weeks unless you say so. Only 50p a week after that one month in advance." He smiled when he read it. He was still laughing at some joke as he put the card in the window. I wasn't. I do need a cleaner, whatever happens, I reasoned.

I was working in a large bookshop in town that stayed open until late. They had a complicated shift system, which meant my times at home were very erratic. I was at home waiting to go in for the afternoon shift when Ms Tidy phoned me. My imagination had ranged from middle aged, with a stage cockney accent, to young and breathless. She was neither; she sounded business-like and spoke BBC. We discussed hourly rates, times. By the time we'd sorted all that out I felt we'd both begun to warm to each other.

Two days later, and I was opening the front door to her. We looked at each other, both trying to recognise someone.

"Hello, you must be Mrs Tidy."

"Hello," she said, "I'm *Ms* Tidy. You're lucky I'm a post-feminist or I'd have your balls off."

I was trying not to shake as I showed her round. I felt like I'd been punched in the guts. She was, quite simply, beautiful. She was funny, friendly and of course I knew I was never going to try it on. She was a real person, not one of Derek's fantasies, and she was way, way out of my league.

We arranged that she would come once a week; the first two weeks I'd definitely be there to show her where everything was and what needed doing. She'd fit in with my shifts. Then she'd come at a time on a Monday to suit her whether I was there or not.

She explained her philosophy of cleaning. "I do have a sense of order, I like trying to get the best out of everything. I'm not OCD. I just can't sit still while other people are making a mess.""

I got used to it. She was chatty. After a few visits I was able to converse without tripping over my own tongue. She was obviously a people person, and she was all ears about who I was and what I did.

"I'm trying to write," I said.

A writer!" she said. "I'm impressed. Are you published?"

"Not yet," I admitted. "I'm working shifts in a bookshop."

"You will be," she said, "when you really want to."

The cleaning was a great success. You can't overestimate the psychological effect of coming home after an awful day at work, the flat smelling all fresh, with a spotless sink in the kitchen and no trace of fluff on the carpet. And she did the ironing, neatly hung up in my wardrobe and filed away with the shirt colours tastefully graded along the spectrum.

"I like cleaning," she told me. "You can actually see what you've achieved in a very short time. So many people work on long projects that never seem to get finished. They get cancelled. You can see the results of cleaning in a couple of hours. You walk into a sordid mess and you leave perfection behind you when you go. People are careless, they don't have time to clean up their messes, they drop things and all the bits get everywhere. Things get covered in dirt and grease. I make their homes worth coming home to. You get all aches and pains, squatting, kneeling, reaching into awkward places. It's not healthy exercise; it's strained muscles and joints, it's sore patches and blisters. But it's never really finished. I get up early, I get to bed late. All over the world there are a million people cleaning and polishing every second." She really had a great mind for a cleaner.

When she was there when I was writing she was supportive and admiring. "Excuse me if I type," I said.

"You deserve to be published," she said, "the work you put into it. Do you mind if I look?"

I overcame my embarrassment and showed it to her. "Not bad," she said. "It could do with a bit of tidying up."

I had to go down to the corner shop to get something for lunch. By the time I got back she'd gone, leaving the smell of polish and sink free of washing-up behind her. I went to my desk – panic! *Where was the stick? Had it fallen off the desk and been sucked up into the vacuum when she did the carpet?*

It was time to leave for the afternoon shift. I hadn't been able to eat the food. At work I paced up and down. *Where was the stick? Why didn't I back up? Why didn't I encrypt things? Why did I never use a password unless I had to?* The customers were even more irritating. The fatuous questions came at me one after the other. "You know, that book by that guy in America. The one with the glasses…"

After a night's sleep I took the flat apart. No sign of the stick. I resigned myself to some toast. The bell rang.

Not Derek again!. But it was her. Ms Tidy. She was smiling and waving a memory stick – *THE memory stick!*

"Have you lost anything?"

"You have saved my life!"

"Don't mention it. I'm sorry – it must have brushed it off your desk into my cleaning stuff."

I read it again. I was very pleased with it. It was even better than I'd remembered it. I got that old feeling that someone else had written it, so it must be good. I sent it off.

A week later my self-addressed envelope was back through the letter box. I tore it open, not expecting much.

What's this – the arrogant bastards! Someone had scribbled corrections all over my manuscript. Then I saw the letter.

"…Perfect story but slightly too long for us. If you can agree to the suggested alterations, we'll take it."

I did exactly as they asked. Six months later it was in print.

After the acceptance my work hours meant that I didn't see Ms Tidy for a month. The success had made me a bit more perky. Maybe she wasn't too good for me…? Should I ask her out for a drink?

I was not above vanity. I started leaving print outs of my stories around so she would see them. But there was no comment, only a scribbled note of the hours she'd worked along with her charges.

It was a month until my morning off coincided with the Monday morning cleaning. I was still jubilant at my success when Mrs Tidy arrived. "I'm really pleased for you," she said when I told her, "but I'm really sorry, you're going to have to find yourself a new Ms Tidy. I'm moving away."

"Have you met someone? Are you getting married?" It was the only explanation that came into my head.

She laughed. "Don't be ridiculous! I've been accepted for the Creative Writing MA at the University of East Anglia."

I sat down with the shock. "You want to be a writer?"

"Yep. I've written three novels and I'm on my fourth. I'm taking this one to the publishers."

"You mean you've written three novels and not tried to publish them?"

"I'd had a cunning plan since I started. I wasn't going to try to get anything published until I felt really good about it. That's the one I take to a publisher and that's my first novel. Then, when they ask for another, I can tidy up one of the old ones. I'll always have something to fall back on if I get writer's block or produce a real dud."

"How long have you known about this?" It was as if I was questioning her about an affair.

"All the time I've been cleaning and saving up. You don't want to end up with more debt than you need. I've got three other jobs. I've done everything. Bar work, shelf stacking. It's no good having a time debt you can't manage."

She was changing before my eyes. A mixture of enthusiasm and anger. "As a cleaner you're always dependent on the whims of others, their times, their schedules. If they move house you lose the gig. Now I'm setting the agenda. We're treated like nothing, but we're essential. Anyway it's been valuable for the writing too. It's really good for people-watching. You find out their dirty little secrets. You get a different view of life from down on your knees. You are *so* shocked, aren't you? It's easy for a cleaner to imagine they can become a writer, but hard for a middle-class person to imagine their cleaner has any talent whatsoever."

After she stopped coming things deteriorated again in the flat. I bought some pyjamas and a television. I started to write in my pyjamas with the telly on. The mess built up. The TV broke. I dumped it in a skip and realised I didn't need another. I flipped between going out and going to bed early, depending on my shifts. Some nights I didn't get back until two in the morning. I often drank alone. I wrote and wrote. I typed neatly when I was sober and scrawled indecipherable squiggles in my notebook when I was drunk. I'd thought Jill was too good for me and I'd thought my own writing was too good for me too. I'd thought Ms Tidy was too good for me and I was right.

I sent everything off, no matter what state it was in. The rejection slips came every time. As the year became unwinnable and hurtled into September, October, I started to wane. I stopped sending everything off except the ones I thought were really good. Then I stopped sending anything off. Then I stopped writing. I wasn't going to stop forever, just long enough to get my flat and my life sorted out. First, I got rid of the traces of Jill that were still lurking. I filled in the Rawlplug holes, painted walls, changed the curtains, carpets, bought pots and pans, lightshades. I stopped binge drinking.

After a lonely Christmas I realised I was in a rut. So I started writing again. I still got the feeling that someone else had written the good stuff, but it wasn't as scary as before.

My long-lost ex, Jill, did come back – once – for Sunday lunch. We'd been apart long enough, we thought, for us to behave like adults, like good friends should, we agreed. The flat was immaculate, I dressed as cool as I could without being obvious. She was at her best perfectly groomed but not flirty.

"This place is SO much better," she said. "You've really improved it." She smiled. "I expect you've improved too – she eyed me up and down – you look great!"

She liked the lunch I'd cooked. She was doing well at work, from Team Leader to Head of Department.

I told her about the published story. She smiled again. "I'm really glad you had a success."

As she was leaving, I thought *I just can't lose her.* I gently caught her at the shoulder, turned her round and stared straight into her eyes. "We must do this again."

She shook her head. "I don't think that would be a very good idea."

I looked a question at her. She nodded.

"Yes, I've met someone. I should have said. We're getting married."

False smiles and false hopes evaporated as I watched her turn the corner of the road.

Derek was at the door. "Your Mrs Tidy" – she's fabulous. I'll take her off your hands"

"*Ms* Tidy. That wasn't her anyway, that was Jill!"

"Good God – she's changed out of all recognition! It really is your loss. Anyway, do you fancy coming to demonstrate for a pedestrian crossing in Monk's Foot road next Saturday."

"Derek…"

"Yes?"

"Fuck off.'

Ms Tidy is certainly published now. I read her stuff. The man in the bookshop said she was honest and competent, he liked it but it was "second eleven stuff" (he was very into cricket) she would never make it big, she wasn't ambitious enough, she didn't have extreme creative fire, she was just too – too – tidy.

But I thought he was wrong. I read all her books and they were all insightful and I was sure she'd go far. There was even a novel about working as a cleaner in South London. But no matter how hard I tried to read between the lines, I couldn't find myself in it. And now I see I was right. I see she's on a well-known short list this year.

I never met anyone to live with. And I've never been published again. I'm in the same flat. I just keep on writing, keep on trying. And Derek still lives over the road in the same flat too. One of his cleaners moved in and they got married eventually. I thought he would have found someone as dire as himself but she's quite normal. At least it means he doesn't come knocking every week. They're both very active in the Residents' Association and they're both standing for the Council.

The biggest change in my life is that I never got another cleaner. I went in for it in a big way myself. I get up early and clean before I go to work. I remember everything Ms Tidy said. You can't underestimate the effect of walking into a spotless home. I've kept up with the decorating, kept up with all the repairs; I feel good when I see it all when I get home from work. I cook myself a nice supper and then I get down to writing almost every evening. It's a wonderful feeling to sit down at a clean tidy desk, with only the story you're writing on it. That way you can really concentrate.

I know I'm going to make it one day. Just like Ms Tidy. I've had one success and I can do it again.

But I won't send this one off; I'll wait till I do something so good it seems someone else has written it.

About the author

Keith Willson, a retired clinical scientist, lives in East Sussex where he performs his poetry and songs. Last year, he completed his MA in creative writing. His work has appeared in *London Magazine, Hot Tin Roof, New Contexts, Pebbles on the Strand, Dream Catcher* and *Scribble.*

Once Upon a Time in America

Nick Padron

Mrs. Blanco has always known she had a smile, sensed it even before she became aware of it. When nothing else would do, her education, her figure, her presence, that simple pull at the ends of her lips speaks with a language of its own. This morning she knows she's going to need it. So sure she is, in fact, that after brushing her teeth, she restrains herself from beaming at the mirror to preserve her smile's full strength.

Outside the window is dusky grey and she reaches for her floral dress, something to brighten up the Monday morning that awaits her. She closes the closet door softly, so as not to wake up her son who's still asleep in the bed they share. From on top of the night table, she picks up her reading glasses next to the *Selecciones del* Readers Digest magazine and slips them on. She wears them all the time now when it's dark.

The long hallways of the boarding house are gloomy silent, her roommates either asleep or gone to work. In the kitchen, she greets Rita, the owner of the *casa de bordantes.* No need to start shining her smile yet. The radio is buzzing the local Spanish news. Mrs. Blanco has her breakfast in between Rita's comments. They're mostly about the weather getting colder. Where Mrs. Blanco comes from *el tiempo* is not much of a subject. It's either raining or it isn't, and usually too hot. Not here, in the city of long coats. The first thing out of people's mouths here, friends or strangers alike, is the weather, how cold is it going to get or what's going to fall from the sky today.

Mrs. Blanco finishes putting on her face by the front door. She reaches into the bottommost of her purse for the keys and locks every lock before she steps away.

It all begins in the elevator, with the simple act of pressing the call button on the wall brass plate. The doors open on their own and she steps inside the mirror and metal box. Her belly shivers as the floor drops, a combination of dread and excitement she's still acquainting herself with since she arrived in New York. Part of the luxury trappings of a past future time, an aging modernity, she is only now catching up to.

For better or worse, everything is temporary. If she is certain of anything it's that. Exile with all its heartbreaks, the same as the guilty enjoyment of a New York elevator ride, is only provisional. The bearded atheists who had forced her and so many to flee her homeland would not keep her forever from the life God had meant her to live.

Outside, it's colder than it looks. She buttons up the winter coat Rita sold her for five dollars and tightens Amelia's red scarf around her neck. As she walks past the store windows in her stiff overcoat, her reflection isn't all that unappealing. It not only conceals her long-lost silhouette and keeps her warm; it also makes her feel part of the landscape, like another New Yorker.

At the bus stop, everyone climbs in one at a time, each dropping a token, unrushed. It is at moments like these too that she's reminded how far she is from home. Tokens instead of money, no one hustling to the empty seats, no conductor to collect the fare. The efficiency of it makes her wonder, though. In her town, buses had a driver and a conductor, and when they'd seen her a few times, she didn't need to signal her stop. Everyone was more in touch with each other, less orderly, sure, but more normal. She wonders how the *americanos*, as smart as they are, could have missed that, the simple human touch.

The downtown bus travels in the shade of Broadway's architecture, a sightseeing show for Mrs. Blanco – and the reason she preferred them to the subway. She presses her forehead on the icy glass window. She grins at the bright storefronts along the way, with their window displays projecting out to the street like movie screens with views of domestic scenes, gleaming kitchenware, and elegant mannequins wearing the latest styles. There's a kind of musical play choreography in the way New Yorkers march across the streets, in the stop-and-go of the vehicle traffic. The grandeur everywhere moves her, the polished sheen of rotating doorways, the assembly lines of yellow taxis, the sheer abundance of affluence. Her faith in the infinite might and wisdom of the *americanos* is reaffirmed at every intersection.

The bus stops at a red light.

When she left Havana, all she and her boy were allowed to bring was $120.00 and – as she liked to say – all the hope and Kleenex they could carry. And, of course, the fervent belief that the United States of America would never allow a Communist nation to take root just ninety miles from Key West. This wasn't only her opinion: everyone she knew was of the same mind. The end of the bearded revolutionaries was only a question of when – maybe a year at the most before she'd be back with her family around her again, back to where she was born and married and had her children, home until three weeks ago.

Today is a particularly difficult day for Mrs. Blanco. It's her first day out looking for a job, in search of employment, something she's never done or needed to do before. At forty-six, the only job she ever had was that of housewife and mother, work that had prepared her for just about anything except to look for employment – much less in a foreign land. The task does not intimidate her as much as the idea of having to ask for it in English, a language she loves to hear but she's incapable of articulating without embarrassing herself.

117

Mrs. Blanco looks at the note her exiled friend, Marta, had given her. "Get off on 34th Street. Walk to 8th Avenue, Garment Center. They're always hiring sewing machine operators in the factories around there," it says.

In Havana, she had a Singer machine with a wrought-iron foot pedal her husband bought her. She'd fashioned dresses and shirts for her children with it when they were younger, even sewn a camping tent for her son's Boy Scout troop once. Sew? Mrs. Blanco could sew just fine.

From the bus, she keeps watch of the street signs at every corner. "Get off when you see the Macy's store and walk around the area looking for Sewing Operator Wanted signs on building walls," Marta's note says.

Many things she never needed before or thought she ever would are needed now. Only a few weeks ago she still lived at home with her husband of twenty-two years and her two children. She'd known the comforts of a well-off existence, which had come with much struggle and only in recent times. But in less than a year of the communist takeover, it was all torn apart, beginning with the seizure of her husband's business, the family house, even the cars. Then came days of desperate rushing around like on a ship in the storm, throwing everything overboard, trying to sell, trade, and hide whatever remained of the family's assets. But the idea of seeking asylum didn't come until later when talk of an even more horrifying law was proposed. The enactment of what they called "Patria Potestad". The law that gave the communist government parental rights over un-emancipated children. Once the rumour took hold, the question of whether or not to leave the country was settled.

The communists could take everything she owns, she decided, but not her son.

Almost overnight, she found herself thousands of miles away, confined to a bedroom in an overcrowded boarding house in New York City with her twelve-year-old son, starting her temporary life of "political" exile, a refugee – a "worm", how the *fidelistas* called the likes of her.

Although the hardships of her younger days now seem like something to look forward to, Mrs. Blanco doesn't allow herself to wallow in her misfortune as some of her fellow exiles do. Hope is fresh yet. Still, the day-to-day is far from easy. Rooming in an apartment full of political refugees is like living with a big wounded, grieving family. Rare is the night that she is not awakened by the muffled sobs of some of her roommates. Exile is the same as living in a permanent state of emergency, ever hanging to a single hope. Every rumour, every word printed or heard on the radio about the homeland has to be dissected, reinterpreted for hidden meanings, every piece of news a new topic to argue about. The one thing the entire exile commune agrees on, though, is, with God and the *americanos* on their side, everything the *comunistas* have stolen from them would be theirs again. And this was something Mrs. Blanco believes with all her heart.

Across the street, on the northbound side of Broadway, Mrs. Blanco notices a sign written in English and Spanish. It speaks of union, employment, and brotherhood. Compelled by a sudden impulse, Mrs. Blanco pulls the cord and gets off the bus and doubles back up the street.

The sweet smell of recently baked dough stops her in her tracks. She rests one hand on the shop window and stares at the trays full of happy-looking donuts arranged in rows. Mentally, she counts the change she has in her purse, hoping. But she knows all too well how much she has, or rather how much she doesn't have, then walks away thinking of all the weight she still could stand to lose – once again looking at the positive side so as not to weep.

She stands under the sign she saw from the bus and takes

up the dark and narrow staircase. At the top landing, she halts by the opened smudged glass door. The air in the grey-walled office reeks of cigarette smoke and indifference. A handful of people are lined up behind a yellow line on the floor, facing a long counter dividing the room.

Mrs. Blanco steps in and surveys the women working behind the counter and at the desks beyond, pecking on their typewriters. A couple of suited men sit behind glass-partitioned cubicles.

She stands with a tentative smile at the end of the line and listens to the English-speaking voice of the bespectacled woman behind the counter, concentrates on it.

The person at the counter walks away and Mrs. Blanco moves up a step.

In front of her, there's a tall black lady and a Latina-looking one who's at the counter now. She's speaking to the bespectacled woman. The harder Mrs. Blanco listens to what they're saying the less she understands.

A minute later, she hears "Next." She remembers what next means. In English, every word sounds so much nicer to her, like in the subtitled movies, the voices of Doris Day, Elizabeth Taylor, and Audrey Hepburn, so musical even when uttered in anger. Yet she's just unable to articulate the words as if her mouth isn't put together the same way as theirs.

The tall black lady steps up to the counter. Mrs. Blanco places the tip of her shoes on the yellow line on the floor. The tall lady seems upset. Something in the document the bespectacled woman handed her has set her off. Her voice is getting louder. She reminds her of those powerful-voiced Protestant preachers in the movies. Mrs. Blanco tries to decipher what each is saying. The noisier they get the less she comprehends them.

The tall woman starts to shake her finger at the impassive

bespectacled face behind the counter. Suddenly she wheels and stomps away, hollering at the entire place. When she reaches the door, she balls up the insulting document, hurls it in the general direction of the wastebasket, and storms out the glass door.

Now the office staff is up, bunched in groups around their desks, ruffled by the irate lady. Mrs. Blanco is up next.

The bespectacled woman waves from the counter. "Come on up."

Mrs. Blanco approaches with a tentative smile: she didn't hear "next". Her throat tightens up. "Pleese, laydee. S-peak S-panish?"

The bespectacled woman turns around and with a cigarette between her fingers waves at someone and walks away.

Spanish Carmen comes to the counter: "How can I help you?"

Mrs. Blanco lets out a sigh of relief and broadens her smile. "Aaayy," she sings out. "Thank God you speak Spanish, *mi hijita*. What a relief."

Spanish Carmen almost smiles.

"Well, the truth is I am looking for work," she says leaning closer to the counter. "Let me explain: I have only been in this country for three weeks, yes. But I am a hardworking person and a fast learner, and I am willing to do whatever work that is being offered."

Carmen gives her a squint-eyed look. "OK, let's see your book."

"*Libro?*" Mrs. Blanco, unsure whether Carmen has understood, starts again. "Maybe I should tell you, I am a married woman. I have two children, yes, two. My oldest, my daughter, she's in Cuba with my husband, *los pobrecitos...* I'm sure you must have heard how terrible things are over there now with those communists taking over, my God. But my son, he's with me. We had to bring him out right away before the communists start taking the children to Russia. Yes, that's another thing those communists are doing. But he's in school now, thank God. And God willing, my husband will be coming to join us very soon. Now, my daughter, we're not too worried about her. She's already eighteen and engaged, yes. She's going to marry a boy we know, a good boy. But in the meantime, well, my son and I have to stay here, you understand, until we can return. So you can imagine how difficult it's been for me to find a job without any English—"

"Excuse me a moment, Mrs. Blan-co, right?"

"Yes," she answers, reaching into her purse for her passport, her ID. "In Cuba, married women get to keep their maiden name, not like here. Yes, it is Blanco."

Carmen, assuming the walk-up is looking for her book, says as she flicks through the Rolodex, "Let's see… We have a few openings for iron operators today. Would that be something you'd want to do?"

"Ironing? Oh, sure. I can iron. My husband tells me no one, not even his mother, can iron his shirts as well as I do."

"All righty, then. Give me your book and I'll send you right out."

Mrs. Blanco hands her passport.

"Not this, your union book, or your card, whichever you brought with you."

"I am sorry *señorita*. I don't have a union book. I could get one if you tell me how—"

"Oh, oh. How can we send you out on a job, if you're not in our union? This is an employment office for our union members. This is not for anybody. I mean you have to be a member."

"No problem, I will join the union. Just tell me how."

"It's not like that. I'm sorry, the jobs we have are for our members in good standing only."

"This is no problem for me. No problem at all. I want to be a union member. Just tell me what I have to do and I will join your union. You see, we just arrived in New York and I need a job—"

"You've already told me, Mrs. Blanco. But I can't send you out unless you're in our union. It's just how it is."

"But I will be very happy to be a member of your union. What is it? Is there a fee?"

"Yes, well no, it's not just a fee. To join our union, you must first work in a union shop for at least three months before you can apply."

"You'll have to pardon me, Carmencita, *chica*. It's a beautiful name, Carmen. I almost named my daughter Carmen, yes. I have a cousin named Carmen too. She's my favourite cousin—"

"Mrs. Blanco…"

"Forgive me, Carmen, I will not bore you with it. But listen, if you give me the ironing job, I promise you I will come back in three months and ask for you personally and I will join your union. A promise is a promise."

Carmen looks over Mrs. Blanco's shoulders at the line. "Look, I'd love to help you—"

"But Carmen, my girl, how can I work for three months and then join the union if you don't give me the job first?"

"These are the rules. I'm really sorry."

"You mean you can't give me a job unless I already have a job?"

"Not really, but in your case, I'm afraid so."

"Why would I come to ask for employment if I am already employed? I'd be too busy at work!"

"I'm sorry. Take this brochure with you. Read it at your leisure. There's nothing else I can do. Next…"

Mrs. Blanco buttons up her coat. "Ay, Carmencita, really. I'm afraid it's going to take me a long time to understand this country." She straps her purse on her shoulder. "To have an employment office for people already employed—" She finished her comment with a silent headshake of disbelieve.

As Mrs. Blanco walks toward the glass door, the heat of emotion wells in her eyes. She halts next to the wastebasket. She looks down at the balled-up paper the screaming lady had shucked with such disdain. Quickly, she lowers herself, picks it up, slips it into her purse and walks out.

Two blocks away, she stops to decipher the words on the paper. It's a printed form filled out with ink but without a bearer's name on it.

"... *Jane Holly Blouses ... West 61st Street ... Steam iron operator ... Salary: $1.25 an hour ... attention: Mr. Weinstein.*"

Her face lights up. She has no reservations in applying for a job a disgruntled member of Carmen's union didn't want. Unions, what are they good for anyway? In Cuba, they called them *sindicatos,* like the one the communists first organized in her husband's factory and then abolished after they confiscated it. But if unions is how the Americans choose to call them, it is fine with her.

On Columbus Circle, Mrs. Blanco runs into a crowd of people waving signs of "JFK for President". She works her way around them and hurries down 60th Street, crosses West End Avenue, and turns on the corner. The Hudson River is just down the road.

A cold wind blows on her face, clean, crisp American air.

61st Street is solid with parked cars. She finds the address. A sign above the doorway says Jane Holly Blouses. She enters the building. Out of the biggest elevator she's ever seen, she encounters a pretty girl at the desk by the door. Mrs. Blanco switches on her smile and hands her the wrinkle-creased but now straightened flat employment form.

The receptionist, chewing gum, picks up a telephone, says one phrase and hangs up, then says something to her and points at a metallic door. The stained sign on it says "Employees Only".

"San-cue," Mrs. Blanco says.

She enters a high-ceiling workshop with long tables. Mr. Weinstein, a thirty-something, pleasant-looking man in a tie and dress shirt, comes walking from behind a stack of rolls of fabrics. The out-turned toes of his shoes are shiny but dusty… a man who doesn't mind getting dirty at work. Mrs. Blanco approves.

She holds out the paper.

Mr. Weinstein doesn't look up at her smile. He scowls at the paper. "Where's your union booklet?"

She answers with her brightest smile something that sounds like this to Mr. Weinstein, "Chess, I lie to goo-erk bery mosh."

He releases a long sigh, steps back, and shouts over the machine noises, "Josefina," then waits, glancing at Mrs. Blanco, sizing her up.

Spanish Josefina, short, with a round cheerful face, races over obviously pleased to be the boss's interpreter.

"Ask Mrs. Blanco if she has her union book or her ID card."

Josefina translates the question.

Mrs. Blanco takes a deep breath and is about to explain why she doesn't yet have a union card when Mr. Weinstein with the out-turned toes cuts her short. "Never mind," he says with a dual expression of pity and mirth on his pale face. "Tell Mrs. Blanco not to worry. Tell her to come back tomorrow at eight in the morning ready to start training. Ironing." He gestures as if waving an iron. "And tell her she'll be starting at a dollar an hour, not at a dollar twenty-five as it says in the form. OK?"

Then Mr. Weinstein adds without the need for translation, louder as if his Spanish would be better understood at a higher volume. "Ma-nya-nah worky on time. OK?"

The message is translated anyway and Mrs. Blanco, beaming, almost curtsies at her new boss. "San cue, bery mosh."

Walking back to the subway, Mrs. Blanco's eyes overflow with tears. She can't believe her luck. To have achieved what only twenty-four hours before seemed like a monumental impossibility feels nothing short of a miracle, as though the Virgin herself was watching over her.

Suddenly, she remembers how hungry she is and picks up her gait. Back in the rooming house, there are hot dogs and a can of Campbell soup waiting for her. Tonight, she announces to herself, she will take her son to the pizzeria on Broadway and celebrate. She slows her pace as she approaches a tumult in Columbus Square.

The crowd is so thick she can't see the end of it. Dozens of JFK for President cardboard signs are up all over the street and over people's heads. Motorcycle policemen are cutting off the traffic. Red lights are swirling. A sudden upsurge of voices and motor noises breaks out and she is dragged by the rushing human tide toward the edge of the sidewalk. A slow-moving black convertible as long as a yacht comes sailing slowly through the mass of bodies. And there, over the sea of outstretched fluttering hands, the figure of John F. Kennedy appears in a royal blue suit, his face under a crown of impeccable chestnut hair, and a smile of perfect white. Drawn by the delirious multitude, Mrs. Blanco reaches out to him as if attracted by an invisible magnet, and their skins clasp together for a magical instant. Then just as quickly, the candidate's caravan floats away.

Mrs. Blanco extricates herself from the mob. She walks away toward Broadway unaware of the importance she would later give to the event. A half-block up 61st Street, she begins to feel faint. She leans on a wall to wait for it to pass. Beside her, there's the tangle of tubes of a scaffold on the side of the building. On a tall windowsill behind her, she sees a neatly folded white paper bag. She takes it and peeks inside. There are two jelly donuts wrapped in wax paper, a capped coffee cup still hot, two sugar packets, a plastic stirrer and paper napkins. She looks around her at the busy sidewalk of incurious New Yorkers passing by. She sighs and puts it back, and walks away.

She halts abruptly, turns back, picks up the paper bag and rushes up the street with it.

On Broadway, she finds a bench in the median promenade. She sits down, pours the sugar into the steaming coffee, and stirs it. Slowly, she takes out a donut. She breathes in its baked aroma and bites the sweet soft dough filled with even sweeter jelly as though performing a delicious but sinful act. Pigeons start gathering nearer. The November sun shines with a silver glow through the overcast Manhattan sky. She savours the donut unhurriedly until is gone except for the white sugary dust on her fingers. She looks into the paper bag, and summoning the phenomenal strength only motherhood could give her, Mrs. Blanco saves the remaining donut for her son.

She gathers herself up and takes the subway uptown.

In her room, she finds her son with his heavy white-sox feet resting on the radiator. He has the transistor radio up by his ear. She drops the groceries on the small table by the door and kisses him on the cheek. He's busy mouthing along with the song playing, mimicking the singer. He's singing in English.

Mrs. Blanco doesn't fool herself by thinking if she ever

went out job-hunting again that she'd be hired the same morning, shake the hand of a presidential nominee, and find a bag with fresh donuts and coffee. But it had happened. And she had done it all on her own. She knew her exiled roommates were going to ask her how her day went, they always ask about everything. She'd have to be watchful of how she told it, Measure her elation, soften the magical aspect of it. Tragedies bring people together, but personal good fortune, not so much. To be an exile, to be forced to flee one's homeland and seek refuge in a foreign country, is like living with an open wound, hurting part of every moment.

Mrs. Blanco approaches her son. His head is bobbing in time with the music. She lets the sweet-smelling paper bag fall on his lap. He drops everything when he sees the donut.

"How did this get here in one piece?" he says, amazed.

"Son, you wouldn't believe the day I had even if I told you."

"Did you find anything?"

Mrs. Blanco smiled.

About the author
Author Nick Padron grew up in New York City. His stories have appeared in numerous literary magazines and anthologies in the US and internationally. He is the author of three novels, The *Cuban Scar*, *The Exhumation* and *Where Labyrinths End*, and a short fiction collection, *Souls in Exile*.

http://www.nickpadron.com

The Changing Pool

Mark Tulin

The congregation engulfed me like a warm blanket. They called themselves loyal servants and embraced me like I was one of them. Each person had a different story to tell, grew up in a different part of the city with unique circumstances, but they all came together for a single purpose. They were to dunk me into a blow-up pool of water and then I was to rise from the water, brand new.

It was the best news any sinner could have. The most loyal attended. I knew only a few of the members personally but I believed that they all loved me. They were proud I was making such a wise choice and was now going to lead a holy life.

I'll never forget that night. It was shortly after my wife left me and abandoned our marriage. The supreme being came to me during my darkest hour: "You have a decision. You can choose Me or the Devil. Which is it?"

"Of course, I choose you, God," I said. "I've been living a devil's lie far too long. It's time to make amends."

There was no drum and bugle corps to highlight the moment. Just the quiet presence in my room. My gloomy world opened up, emptying out all the darkness and pain. No more sadness or grief. No more resistance to the truth.

I spilled my anti-depressants down the toilet and cancelled my psychiatry appointments. I tossed an ounce of hash into the garbage and got rid of my prized rock collection. I removed all of the symbols of secularity that got me into trouble, breaking my Laughing Buddha and tearing my tarot cards in two. The things that I felt were important no longer mattered.

When the big day arrived, I was ready. I said my prayers, read several passages from King James and had a light pre-baptismal breakfast consisting of oatmeal and strawberries.

A few hours later, I found myself in the middle of a plastic, inflatable swimming pool in the rear of a little red-brick church. It was a beautiful May afternoon. A few robins were chirping and a dog barked in a neighbour's backyard.

When Pastor Joe appeared, he placed one hand on my back and another held the King James as we stood in waist-deep water. People huddled around the pool, standing patiently with lit candles, smiling like they were about to witness a miracle.

I already felt clean. No more judgment and rejection. Hardships were a thing of the past. Now, I was a shining star with a couple dozen friends by my side. All I had to do to complete this change was lean back into the water.

I trusted Pastor Joe. He was the closest thing to an angel. His eloquent sermons make me cry and repent. His six-foot-three body stood in the pool, announcing how pleased he was that I had chosen this day to be saved.

He wore a Kelly green sweatshirt with a silver cross around his neck. He had a red Phillies cap on top of a few strands of hair. He's presided over at least fifty baptisms and each one was special.

He cleared his throat and asked me a question in a pastoral tone: "Do you trust Him with all your heart?"

There was no pause, no indecision. I was ready to devote my life to the righteous and let go of the immoral.

"Yes!" I shouted.

My body quivered and twisted as a holy chill shot through me. I floated backward in slow motion, feeling an angel with soft wings holding me, allowing my body to settle into the silence of the pool.

As I slowly entered the water, I felt everything change

– my mind clearing, a softness coming over my face, and every muscle in my body relaxing. I saw myself from above, submerged four feet under, with Pastor Joe cradling my head in his reassuring hands.

"I baptize you in the name of the Holy Spirit."

I opened my eyes and saw the people's blurry faces through the water, holding candles with the darkening sky above their heads.

The water was as warm as my body temperature, comforting me like a mother taking me in her arms, coddling my nakedness.

I couldn't wait any longer. I didn't want to go back to my mortal life, but wanted to go to heaven. *Please*, I implored, *take me without delay. Let me sit beside you at the throne.*

The longer I lay in the soothing pool in the presence of the spirit, the more I wanted to die. I wanted death's hand to squeeze the breath out of me, to wring out of all my filthy humanness and corruption and made me a spirit in the sky.

In the midst of my serenity, nearing a most peaceful surreal state, Pastor Joe abruptly lifted me out of the water and wrapped a towel around my shoulders.

The congregation hooted and hollered. They called out things like, *brand new! You're saved!*

They didn't see the disappointment on my face or the reluctance in getting out of the pool. They waited to hear my words of appreciation, expecting me to say the right things so they could applaud and rejoice in my good news.

A gospel singer strummed his acoustic guitar. My hair was dripping wet, hanging loosely over my eyes. My head was spinning like a top. I could barely see the people's melting faces swirling around me. All my thoughts were back in the baptismal pool where I felt safe and warm.

"I now baptize you in the name of our father," Pastor Joe said. "Buried with Him in the likeness of His death, raised with Him in his likeness… to walk in the newness of life."

The singer strummed his guitar louder. The congregation called out un unison, *Testimony! Testimony!*

The warmth of the water and the divine beckoned me. The church and its congregation were alluring but deceiving. Don't they want me to be truly happy? I felt pity for everyone, including Pastor Joe who wouldn't let me be with the creator. I yearned for the stillness of the water.

Then I spoke. The crowd went silent.

"I was contemplating suicide when my wife left. Then out of nowhere the Holy One appeared. All I could do was humble myself before God, kneel down and ask for a new life."

The congregation cheered, raised the candles to the sky and chanted: "Blow the trumpet in Zion! Sound the alarm in the valleys and on the mountaintops!"

My mind kept going back to the water. I felt lifeless there, breathless, and beautifully empty.

Pastor Joe had other plans. When I was in the water, he pulled me out because he believed it was the right thing to do. But he didn't know how much pain I was in or how long I had suffered. I couldn't pass up this opportunity to go out in front of my friends.

I let go of his hand and jumped back into the pool, catching everyone by surprise. This time, there were no angels bracing my fall. I flopped in the pool like a heavy anchor, sinking fast to the blue, vinyl bottom. I didn't hold my nose or shut my mouth but sucked in all the water. I allowed the warm liquid to flow down my windpipe and nostrils, filling me up from head to toe like a giant water balloon. I welcomed every drop of the pool water, letting the spirit permeate through me, saturating my pores, washing away my past. I wanted to disappear in the clear translucence, to become a mist, free and invisible, and then to swirl-up like a holy ghost to heaven.

Bare feet, different sizes, some with shoes stepped into the pool. These were a dozen or so church members who desperately tried to yank me out of the water.

"Pull the plug!" someone yelled.

There was no joyous applause, just male arms in struggle. But I was much stronger than they expected. I clutched tighter to the pool liner, gripping my fingers to the thin plastic undercoat, holding on as long as I could. I felt the sweet water rushing inside of me, bathing my lungs, filling my stomach, and surrounding my soul.

A woman's shrill voice read a prayer for the dead. She prayed that my soul rise to a higher realm: "May He create peace in death for this young man."

I kept repeating – *The water is love. It is my absolution. It is kind, clean, and true*.

Several members of the congregation screamed: *Call 911! Call 911!*

Panic took over the little red brick church and the neighbourhood.

My death was unexpected. They've seen hundreds of baptisms but none like this. This was never supposed to happen, they thought, and then they let out a collective gasp when my body floated to the surface of the pool and the men picked me up and placed me on the grass.

CPR was useless. They were powerless in the face of death, just as I was powerless in my life. The candles flickered-out and the only light that shone was the glow from the moon and the whites of my eyes.

About the author

Mark Tulin is a former therapist from Long Beach, California. A publisher compared his work to artist Edward Hopper on how he grasps people's peculiar traits. Mark's books include *Magical Yogis, Awkward Grace, The Asthmatic Kid and Other Stories, Junkyard Souls, Uncommon Love Poems,* and *Rain on Cabrillo.* Mark appeared in *Amethyst Review, Books 'N Pieces, EveryWriter, Spillwords, Fiction on the Web,* and others. He is a Pushcart nominee and Best of Drabble. Find Mark at:
https://crowonthewire.com
https://mftulin.medium.com
@Crow_writer

The Day Internet Died

Boris Glikman

It was widely known that Internet had been ailing for some time. Its poor health had made it rather slipshod in the execution of its duties. Some had to endure days of frustration until an online connection was established, while for others the connection kept going on and off every second, like a flickering light bulb.

For a while Internet hovered in a half-dead condition, with one foot in the offline eternity, and mankind held its breath, fearing Internet would continue to deteriorate and then give up the ghost altogether.

And then the day came when Internet breathed its last and no one could believe their ill fortune. It was hard to grasp that Internet no longer dwelled in the world, and that the burden of living would never again be lightened with the ever-present alternative of escaping into an online existence. No longer would anyone be privileged with the luxury of having two worlds to live in.

The most eminent computer technicians of the land were assigned the task of performing the autopsy. Their unanimous conclusion was that Internet had died of virtual causes. What no one had suspected was that the Internet possessed a finite life span. Everyone had always assumed it would be around forever, yet it too carried within itself the lethal seeds of eternal offline-ness.

The next most pressing issue was the burial. Issues never considered before needed to be urgently addressed, for the sight of lifeless Internet lying prostrate on the ground was too heart-breaking for the world to take. Where should the funeral ceremony be held? In which language or computer code should the memorial service be conducted? Who should give the eulogy? Where to entomb it?

The matter of whom to invite to the service proved to be the most intractable issue of all. A certain number of tickets were reserved for those most deeply affected by Internet's death – online pornography addicts, social misfits, ingrained introverts, Twitter-obsessed celebrities, the heirs of Nigerian princes and long term residents in Second Life's virtual world. Otherwise, it was nearly impossible to determine who was genuinely grief-stricken and who only wanted to attend the ceremony so as to be a part of this historic occasion.

Eventually, all of these matters were resolved, although not to everyone's satisfaction, and the world gave Internet the sending off it deserved. Straight after the funeral, the world went into a shutdown, mourning Internet's passing and remembering wistfully how it could answer any question, satisfy all emotional, mental, spiritual, intellectual and bodily needs, thrill the mind and the senses, provide instantaneous information, entertainment, relaxation, gratification and titillation, as well as enabling instant communication with people across the globe, and even cure loneliness. Tragically, given the magnitude and depth of the loss, some could not bear to continue living in a world without Internet and logged out permanently from this world.

Once the unbridled, hysterical wave of grief finally subsided, mankind sobered up and gradually came to realise that Internet had actually debased and disfigured their lives.

They recalled with horror and consternation the way Internet had ensnared people with its myriad tentacles, causing them to waste their lives away in the inextricable morass of the net world; how googling had supplanted the wisdom that comes with age, experience, learning and how, with instantaneous information always at one's fingertips, the value of knowledge was lost, and the way online reality became the only world and real reality was jilted and forgotten, just like the plain sister of a gorgeous girl. They remembered how Internet robbed life of its multifarious richness and beauty and reduced the world to a small, rectangular screen, and the way the online world became a prison in which humanity willingly immured itself and then threw away the key, together with their lives.

Mankind now recognised how Internet had fundamentally altered the nature of social relations and the nature of one's relationship with oneself. Invented to facilitate communication and for bringing the world together, Internet instead became the perfect tool for dissimulation, distorting the truth and separating oneself from the world, thus allowing people to not only misrepresent their true thoughts and feelings, but to falsify their entire lives and the very essence of their being, to others as well as to themselves.

People discovered that fingers were not just for typing and shifting mouses but had other uses too, that out of their torsos there extended a pair of lower limbs which could be used for perambulating across the spatial dimension, that Evolution had equipped their bodies with the ideal means of conveying thoughts and feelings, that their faces possessed well-developed muscles which could be employed to signal emotions such as (amongst many others) surprise, annoyance, happiness and frustration. Consequently, successful communication could be achieved without intermediary electronic devices. Most startling of all was the revelation that other people were not identical to their icons – flat and forever stuck in the same pose with the same smile on their faces – rather they were three-dimensional beings, moving about and changing their facial expressions.

Having friends and partners in the physical world meant

you were free from the precariousness, uncertainty and unreliability of online friendships and relationships, and no longer subject to the capricious actions and decisions of your web pals, to whom, after all, you were just an ethereal, abstract entity that could be deleted instantly and permanently from their life with just a click of a mouse. Consequently, the constant threat of online friends and lovers inexplicably ceasing all contact and disappearing forever was gone for good.

"Back to Reality" tutorials proved to be very popular and helpful, covering such topics as "Learning How to Single-Task", "Becoming Acquainted with the Sun and the Sky" and "How to Survive in a World that Cannot be Photoshopped".

Life slowly regained its meaning as mankind clambered, one small step at a time, out of the online abyss it had dug for itself. Without Internet, no one had to grapple any more with the problem of how to balance one's life between the two worlds. Time started to flow more slowly. Instant gratification was no longer craved. Contemplation and patience revealed their true worth. It was now clearly seen that online reality provided only fleeting pseudo-meaning, that emotions felt in the web world were only ephemeral artificial feelings, and that real self-esteem came not from social media popularity, but from within.

Each human being now experienced life directly, rather than through the distorting, diminishing and vicarious lens of a computer screen. Mankind faced the good and the not-so-good things in their lives without escaping into the net world, and thus evading the reality of their existence. People became true to their inner selves, no longer hiding behind their icons and online identities.

Only then was it realised how deeply and intricately

Internet had woven its fateful thread into every aspect of man's existence and how much had been gained the day Internet died.

About the author

Boris Glikman is a writer, poet and philosopher from Melbourne, Australia. He says: "Writing for me is a spiritual activity of the highest degree. Writing gives me the conduit to a world that is unreachable by any other means, a world that is populated by Eternal Truths, Ineffable Questions and Infinite Beauty. It is my hope that these stories of mine will allow the reader to also catch a glimpse of this universe."

The End of the Beginning

S. Nadja Zajdman

*Now this is not the end. It is not even the beginning
of the end. But it is, perhaps, the end of the beginning.*
Winston Churchill, November 10, 1942

It was midnight, and silent. Mannheim had not known a silent midnight in two years. Skulking in the bushes beyond the ruins of the *Rathaus*, Renia bid her time. The lights inside American Military Government headquarters were out; the moonless sky was black. Seizing the moment, Renia dashed across the grounds and raced along the flowerbed...

A jeep carrying two G.I.s sped through the debris of the devastated streets and screeched to a halt in front of an apartment that Chaplain Hasselkorn requisitioned for three Polish Jews who had passed on false papers. A young man and two young women, one, still in her teens, had been brought to him six weeks before by a Jewish G.I. The younger girl was caught in last-minute cross-fire while foraging for food. Crouching for cover in the rubble of a gutted home, she overheard a soldier trying to communicate with a German civilian in a guttural language, she knew, was not German. She waited for the G.I. to finish speaking. She skirted around the scraps of metal and loose bricks that littered the devastated streets, and ran after him.
"*Jude!*" She shouted.
The soldier bristled. "What?"
"*Jude!*" Renia pleaded, pointing at him. The soldier glowered. "Who the fuck are you?!"
"*Jude! Ich bin Jude,*" Renia insisted, first, in desperation, and then with a resurfacing sense of hope.

140

"Oh Jesus!" Finally, light dawned. "You…?"

"Ja! Jude! Jude! Ich bin Jude!" Renia beamed, fervently shaking her head.

"Oh Christ!" The Jewish G.I. gasped in recognition.

"Kom." Renia led the overwhelmed soldier to a cylinder along the riverbank in which two people huddled together. Slave labourers were denied access to German bomb shelters. Her friends Cesia and Shimon cowered inside. Renia spoke to them in Polish and gently coaxed them out.

The G.I. brought the three young people to the American Military Government headquarters, to Chaplain Hasselkorn. Chaplain Hasselkorn promptly ejected a German couple from a nearby apartment, and bequeathed the space to Cesia, Shimon, and Renia. Now they were standing at the apartment entrance.

"Hi!" The driver winked. "You guys ready?"

Cesia, Shimon, and Renia glanced at each other. Cesia wore a dress, and Shimon, a suit that Renia had "requisitioned" from the closet of the departing German couple. Renia wore a dyed white coat over her own dress, which she had converted from a khaki-coloured American army blanket. Designated the group's spokesman, Renia stepped up and responded, "Och Kay! Ve ready!"

"Well hop in!" The driver thumbed towards the back of the jeep. Renia turned to her companions, showing off her constantly expanding English vocabulary. "Okie Dokie. Let's go!"

Carefully, Shimon lifted Cesia into the jeep. She was carrying his child. Renia followed, carrying the bouquet she'd assembled from the contents of the flowerbed in front of the old *Rathaus.*

The G.I.s drove out of the city and onto the *Autobahn* to Heidelberg. Heidelberg had been unharmed on orders from

141

General Eisenhower because he planned to install his headquarters there. Jewish G.I.s had stumbled upon a tiny synagogue in a narrow lane in Old Heidelberg that, curiously, was still standing. The jeep clattered over the cobblestones of the ancient town, and rode up to it. Inside, a buffet table was heaped with doughnuts, cold cuts, pretzels, jelly beans, Wrigley's chewing gum, O'Henry chocolate bars, wine, beer, Ginger Ale, cola and Florida oranges the size of sunsets. The G.I.s had obtained the food in much the same manner as Renia had obtained the bouquet.

Renia and her companions gaped. They had not seen such a feast in six years. "Take a load off. Relax!" While the soldiers added final touches to the table, Renia and her companions sat on the synagogue steps, and waited. An hour later, a canvas truck, flanked by a jeep, rumbled up the road. Chaplain Hasselkorn, accompanied by a pair of United Nations Relief and Rehabilitation Administration workers, leapt out and pulled the canvas aside. Wraith-like apparitions began to stir. The U.N.N.R.A. workers stretched out their arms, and skeletal hands latched onto them. Laboriously these spectres limped off the truck, their steps tentative, unsteady, like pencils attempting to walk. They'd been liberated from their striped camp uniforms, deloused, scraped clean, and then dressed in an assortment of ill-fitting and mismatched clothes. One by one, the figures filed off the back of the truck. There were thirty of them; all men. They were confronted by a shy young couple almost as emaciated as they were, and a grinning teenager cradling a long-stemmed bouquet in her arms. She was robust and rosy-cheeked, having already benefited by Seventh Army largesse. Instinctively, the silhouettes knew.

"*Amchu?*" they whispered, to the couple, and the girl.

"*Amchu,*" the three affirmed. One of us… There were still Jews in the world. There were still Jewish women.

Their own women had been wrenched from them at the first selection. Was there a wife or a sister who had been spared? Were such miracles possible? How?

Rabbi Hasselkorn led the congregation into the synagogue. Shimon and Cesia were pronounced man and wife.

After the ceremony, the congregation gathered around the buffet table. The bridal couple, the maid of honour, and the guests, in a daze, exchanged tales of survival. Tears, dammed for years, flowed like champagne. The men were Polish Jews from a town called Radom. They had been deported together and had survived, together. Five weeks earlier they had been liberated at Vaihingen by the French. They had been placed in a village near Neuenberg, and were beginning to recover. However, the French commander in charge of the village had received orders to transfer them to a Polish D.P. camp, and he had been concerned about the treatment Jewish survivors were likely to receive there. He had approached Chaplain Hasselkorn, who had approached a Jewish lieutenant from Chicago, who had succeeded in having the Radomer Jews transferred to the American zone because his superior looked away.

The Radomer Jews were currently housed in an ancient castle down the road. The lieutenant had evicted squatting Germans, Ukrainians, and Latvians, had the castle cleaned, and the Radomer Jews moved into *Schloss Langenzelle*. Now they were attending a wedding reception. Only those capable of digesting solids, and strong enough to stand, had been invited to the wedding. The flesh of oranges, peeled by trembling fingers, erupted like sunbursts. Doughnuts, sprinkled with real sugar, sparkled like jewels on reverently held paper plates. With their treasures, the men shuffled to the wooden benches in the centre of the room. One of their number, a young man called Kaddish, moved to the front, to where the *bimah* had once been. Without prompting, without accompaniment, he sang Kol Nidre. *"All personal vows we are likely to make, all personal oaths and pledges we are likely to take between this Yom Kippur and the next Yom Kippur, we publicly renounce. Let them all be relinquished and abandoned, null and void, neither firm nor established. Let our personal vows, pledges and oaths be considered neither vows nor pledges nor oaths."* As Kaddish's clear tenor filled the hall, the gathering grew hushed. Heads were bent in contemplation; shoulders were stooped in sorrow. Kaddish concluded the prayer. Palms plunged into eye sockets as if, by so doing, they could press out memory.

Slowly the congregation rose and moved outside, into the courtyard. The sky was silver. The stones glistened. It was drizzling. An U.N.R.R.A. worker pulled out a *Leica* camera. "O.K. Gang. One for the album." The congregation arranged itself into three rows: Shimon and Cesia in the middle, with Rabbi Hasselkorn standing next to the bride. The front row was kneeling. Renia perched on a soldier's lap. Kaddish sat on the damp earth, next to her. Renia would meet him again, in Canada, at her own wedding. He would become her brother-in-law. The U.N.R.R.A. worker aimed the lens. "Come on everybody. SMILE."

The group gazed into the May mist. Beyond their vision lay a maze of roofs caught between the river and the hills. They stared out from this fairytale town, nestled within a gorge, untouched by horror, atrocity, nor even time. The mountains hung on the horizon, and a train chugged along the banks of the Neckar: *the trains... the trains... The* group stared into an open future and, bravely, smiled.

About the author

S. Nadja Zajdman is a Canadian author. In 2022 she published the story collection *The Memory Keeper* (Bridge House Publishing, Manchester) as well as the memoir *I Want You To Be Free* (Hobart Books, Oxford). In 2023 she followed up with a second memoir, *Daddy's Remains* (MacKenzie Publishing, Canada). In 2022, 2023 and 2024 Zajdman's work was selected for inclusion in Bridgehouse's annual anthology *The Best of CaféLit*. At the end of 2024 Bridgehouse brings out Zajdman's essay collection *Between Worlds*.

The Hymn of the Bees

Andrea Stephenson

It was an old hymn that led me back here. I must've overheard it on the street. I don't remember, but I found myself humming it. Couldn't get the damn tune out of my head. And suddenly here I was. I should've known where I was going, should've remembered the way, but a lot's changed since I was a kid. Seems like centuries ago. Used the last of my cider money for the bus fare; God knows why. The bus driver wrinkled his nose up at me but I glared him down; my money's as good as anyone else's. I wish I hadn't now. I could do with a drink to keep me warm.

They've done the old farmhouse up, put in double glazing, given it a lick of paint. Light spills out onto the snow, warm orange light that makes me shiver. Two gleaming cars in the driveway. I can't see anyone moving about in there, but I can imagine them, a nice shiny family sitting around the Christmas tree that's sparkling in the window. Ours was always a straggly thing, with wonky lights and threadbare tinsel. There were never many presents under it.

The fields are gone of course. There's a strip of green around the house so it still feels country, but it's surrounded by a smart new estate. The village isn't a village anymore. It's got a Tesco and a McDonalds and a Costa Coffee. There are houses where the old barn used to be. Can't say I'm sorry it's gone. We should've burned it down ourselves after that night.

I should've expected that the hives wouldn't be here anymore. It was over forty years ago. But I really hoped someone would've saved them. Might as well stay now anyway, won't be long until midnight.

"Santa?"

I jump at the shrill voice.

I turn around to see a child. I'm not sure how old. I was never any good at children. I can't imagine why she'd mistake me for Santa. I fluff up my tangled white hair and look down at my red coat, so filthy it's more like a dark plum. Maybe from the house you could confuse me with the old feller, maybe in the dark… but I'm not that old and I'm definitely not that fat.

"Go away," I say. "You should be in bed." I check my watch; I can just see the numbers behind the cracked face. Ten to midnight. I glance uneasily at the house. I don't want some angry parent marching out and warning me away from their precious child. My feet are sodden. I'm freezing. I don't know why I'm still here. I wish I had some cider to warm me up.

"You're not Santa!" the girl says. I'd forgotten for a minute that she was there.

"No, I'm not bloody Santa."

She gasps. I think she's going to cry. She looks very small in her pyjamas and fluffy slippers. At least she's got a coat on.

"You live here?" I try to soften my voice and after a minute she nods.

"Well, I used to live here too," I say. I have an urge to tell her. To tell her about the last good memory. Me and my brother. Not much older than she is, I think. Slipping out of the house near midnight on Christmas Eve, but not to look for Santa.

There were six hives here then. When everything else was falling apart we still had the bees.

The clock startles me. The church is a few miles away but the night's crisp and clear and the sound always did carry. I lift my head up and close my eyes, listening to the chimes of midnight. Afterwards, the silence rings. I wait, but of course there's nothing. There aren't any bees here anymore. My legs give way then. I thunk into the snow, too cold to notice the way it freezes me. My face is wet and I realise I'm crying. It's been a long time since I've cried, when I'm sober anyway.

This was never really a happy home. The farm always hanging by a thread. Dad always weighed down by the threat of going bust and Mam spinning out just enough from too little. I always knew what a gun meant. It was a rabbit for the pot, an animal that was sick or too old, a flock of crows scared away from the crops. But that night it was something else. That night it was the spatter of Dad's blood on straw. It was the smell of shit and desperation.

The girl is tugging my shoulder. She's holding something out to me in hands tinged blue with cold. A battered mince pie in one, a small glass of brandy in the other. I sniff, wipe my hand roughly over my eyes.

"Are they not for Santa?" I ask. She shrugs and smiles.

I'm careful not to snatch the glass, but I drink it in one go, then stuff the pie in my mouth. My body shudders and I struggle to stand. She watches me closely while I stamp my feet and brush snow off my legs.

"On Christmas Eve, the bees sing," I say. She looks puzzled and I wonder why I'm telling her this.

"Just after midnight, they hum a tune. A hymn for... Baby Jesus. He's just been born you know."

She nods, uncertain. "There used to be bees here," I say, shrugging. I look back at the empty space and wonder what happened to them. How long did they last after we'd gone? It was Mam who first told us the legend. Mam who would lead us down here on Christmas Eve. And the bees never let us down.

"Anyway," I sniff, "I'd better go and you need to get

back to bed before anyone notices you've gone." She gives me a mischievous smile and I find myself smiling back at her. I turn away from the place the bees once were, ready to walk away for the last time. I can't think why I ever came.

But just as I turn, there's a hitch in the air. Something heard but not heard. It's very faint, but the snow makes sounds bigger. I turn back and – yes – I hear it, the hint of familiar notes. I push off, into the trees, stumbling in banked snow, ignoring the scratch of branches. It gets louder and louder, until my head is filled with humming. And then I see it: the swarm. A big, fat teardrop hugging a tree. They shouldn't be swarming at this time of year, they should be tucked up in a hollow keeping their queen warm and safe for the winter. But they aren't. They're here, and the whole tree vibrates with their song.

I feel a nudge and the girl is beside me.

"Can you hear them?" I ask.

She nods, eyes wide. We stand listening, not feeling the cold anymore. At some point, she puts her hand in mine and, just for a minute, she's my brother. Mam and Dad are there too and we're all listening to the hymn of the bees as if nothing bad will ever happen to us. All too soon the humming fades, oozing into silence. For a minute, everything is still, then the bees take flight in a commotion of buzzing. I watch the murmur of the swarm as it passes overhead and seeps into the darkness.

I walk the child back up to the house. She waves as she creeps inside. She still believes in magic. Still believes in the safety of a warm bed. I hoist my sleeping bag onto my shoulders. If I'm lucky I'll find an empty bus shelter to bed down in for the rest of the night. I don't believe in magic. And I know that what seems like a home can be swept away in a single desperate act. I believe in the magic of cider to make me forget and to keep me warm. But that hymn is still marching around my head. I look at the house for the last time, down to the shadows at the bottom of the garden. The bees came. Bees where no bees should have been and a song that no-one should have heard. Maybe, just maybe, somewhere in the woods, there's a bit of magic left that I can believe in.

About the author
Andrea is a writer and Library Manager from the North East of England, where she lives with her wife and a Border Terrier. Her stories have been published in *Toasted Cheese, Firewords, Popshot* and a number of anthologies. She writes about nature, the seasons and magic at harvestinghecate.wordpress.com. She is currently seeking publication for two novels for adults.

The Liberations of Cassie Youmans

Norman Thomson

Cassie Putman was thinking of a forthcoming week away in Quebec City, and her choice of frocks for dinner wear when the office accountant Jim Elmond strode into her office and planted himself across from her desk.

"I know what you've been doing," he said. "How often, how much, and how long."

Anger and disappointment hardened his face. Cassie's stomach tightened.

He waved the sheaf of papers in his right hand. Cassie saw it as a bludgeon smashing into her life, scattering her work, her reputation, her circle of friends into instant ruin. She was too startled to cry.

Cassie gripped the edge of her desk to quiet her trembling. A dark hole loomed in front of her. She looked into Jim Elmond's eyes. Hesitantly at first, then with growing assurance she admitted to her pattern of petty thefts. "It's stupid behaviour. Criminal, of course. Don't ask me why, because I don't know. I really don't." She had no thought on offering any of several excuses or rationalizations, gambling or alcohol addiction or creeping debt. "I always wanted to stay with the piddling amounts. Things get ahead of you and before you know it, you've lost control."

Elmond remained silent. Cassie studied him, eager for a cue to continue.

"So… what next? You can prosecute, and send me to jail. Or terminate me, and hope any lingering scandal will disappear."

Elmond scanned Cassie's face to ascertain emotion or motive there. "What would you do, in my place?"

"I can't answer that. I know what I want you to do now."

"Tell me."

"Give me the chance to turn this thing around. Let me pay it back. All the money I... stole. There, I've said it. I can make it good. Please, Mr. Elmond. Just give me a chance." She loosened her grip on the desk. "I swear I'll make this right."

"I'll sleep on it tonight. We'll sort it in the morning."

Next day Jim Elmond told Cassie she could depend on his cooperation and they would arrange a means of repayment, with strict oversight. The following day he left for one of his habitual long-distance holidays, this one to Thailand.

The subject of Mr. Elmond's travel destinations was at first a running source of amusement, speculation and mystery for the staff of Ballantrae. [*Fine Furniture. Since 1916.*] Not for him the standard Caribbean all-inclusives or Vegas casinos. Instead, he sought exotic places, temple communities of Cambodia: remote villages in India. Sometimes he would comment on the lure of spiritual calm or welcoming locals to be found there. It was after his return from a getaway to northern India that he attended the wedding of Carl Youmans, third generation owner of Ballantrae Furniture, and Cassie Putman.

For eighteen months Cassie and Jim Elmond kept a bond of silence between them on the subject of her dipping. Cassie refused to pull married rank at the factory. She made it a point of honour to set aside a portion of her weekly pay and Christmas bonus to reimburse all the stolen funds. One crisp November morning Elmond told her any hidden debts to the firm were ancient history and we won't give it another thought.

Two weeks after celebrating their twenty-fourth anniversary, Carl collapsed dead in the factory milling room. His silver beard was dusted with wood shavings. Cassie was twelve days shy of her fifty-first birthday.

She dream-walked through the funeral and early grieving. She pulled back from her walking club outings. Gina Martin from Marketing took her under her wing to offer company and occasional county Arts Trail explorations. "You and Carl shared some wonderful years," Gina said. "And raised two happy, successful children." Cassie imagined her daughter Naomi, teaching English in Zambia, coping with curious chickens wandering into her open classroom. Of her son Andrew, a driven grasping realtor in Vancouver, she gave little thought.

She found herself idling inattentively through the orders books, content to leave day-to-day affairs to Jim Elmond. When the sluicing sound of the close by Macklin river wafted into her office she wanted to jog along the bordering asphalt path and feel her leg muscles firm up. Her bridge partners urged her to sell her company share to Mr. Elmond, and get on with her life. But privately she feared falling on hard times. It would destroy her to look again to Jim Elmond for rescue from an unpleasantness of her own making.

Cassie could not determine the precise time when thoughts of remarrying stole into her mind. She saw the business sputtering along, losing profit to cheap foreign imports. She was increasingly dissatisfied at being the odd one out at social functions. Though she worried herself over deepening lines about her eyes and mouth, she was attractive still, she told herself. She was energetic for new experiences, travel or music or craft related. Beside which, she still kept a strong desire for male companionship. She missed the sounds of Carl's deep voice echoing throughout the house. As for eligible partners, she saw only a dreary landscape ahead. Online dating sites frightened her. The office women had related horror stories of lurking, needy men. In her tramping

153

club there was Gerald Summers, a lifelong bachelor who lived with his aged mother. And Major Duffy, who dressed himself sloppily and often drank too much. There was no one else, except perhaps Jim Elmond, with his upright bearing and sober manners. Cassie sometimes wondered what he did for fun away from the factory, apart from his exotic trips abroad. Even now she could not think of Elmond without a burst of shame at her earlier indiscretions. She admired his forthrightness when he spoke to her of the Chinese enquiries.

"We have a promising offer from a Shanghai firm to buy the business, lock-stock. Solid financing, good payment terms and close to market value." He hesitated. "Which, sad to say, isn't a great deal at this stage."

Cassie wanted to shout her joy at this unexpected turn. "Will you highlight the details for me? And Jim, keep in mind staff protection and security, please? Carl would have kept their interests uppermost."

She had a sudden urge to lace on her runners and jog several miles along the river track.

Gales of laughter rose along the grassy slopes of the picnic area. Roland Hawksworth had told a joke about three elderly women arriving at the Pearly Gates, only to meet there a defrocked priest. Marjory Hawksworth, who had turned an ankle during the morning's tramp and wanted sympathy for that soreness, cautioned him against telling another. Portly Major Duffy announced that he was famished and let's set out the pot luck food trays.

Ron Hoover, the retired physician, queried her about the Chinese offer. She had forgotten about the factory, taking her pleasures from the sight of a curious fox watching them from nearby shadows. She felt suddenly alone and unfit.

Major Duffy offered her a plate with a scoop of potato

salad and cucumber slices. "Dig in, Cassie. Lots to go around." Having overheard the reference to the factory, Duffy said, "I hear Jim Elmond is scouting around for prospects when the foreign buyers move in. He'll manage okay."

Everyone liked Jim Elmonds. He was amusing and genial at staff parties and liked to converse about economic trends worldwide. Cassie admired his sense of travel adventure. It might be pleasant to wander the bazaars of Morocco, or traverse the glaciers of Iceland in Jim's company. He'd provide security and companionship. With his experience, he'd be able to organize travel plans and straighten glitches easily.

Shortly after noon on alternate Sundays during the summer months Jim Elmond drove himself in his engineer's costume, striped overalls with full bib, and red bandana, to Sanderson Park, where he took his seat on the locomotive of the Sanderson Miniature Railway. Sunlight sparked off the fresh green paint along the side plates and over the polished brass registration numerals. He gave two warning calls from his engine whistle. Behind him, three passenger carloads of children whooped their readiness.

Their journey took them in a lazy, half mile oval pattern. They skirted a pond edged with flowering white lily pads. The rhythmic clatter of the wheels brought into his mind the rattle of the power saws in the factory cutting room. He would miss the work routine, would miss the people in the office and on the shop floor. With many, he knew their lengths of service, their children's names, even some present medical anxieties.

The train chuffed through a small meadow. Where would he be when the new buyers moved in. There's been no mention of their keeping staff on. And really, sixty-three is too young to retire, with no sizeable pension for support. Cassie will be all right if she can keep herself clear of unscrupulous "advisers" who want to be lining their own pockets. How might he broach the subject of wise investing to her, give of his expertise and experience to safeguard her assets?

He slowed the train as it approached the platform. Smiled as the disembarking children thanked him for "an awesome ride, and keeping the train on the tracks".

The numbers were grim and unassailable. Compiled in Elmond's elegant lettering, neat columns narrated her and the factory employees' declining prospects. It's was tearing Carl's lifetime's work away and all their dreams with it.

"Take out severance packages and holiday allowances, settle with the suppliers, and the capital fund looks rather lean," she said.

"The house and cars are not attached to the factory," Elmond said. "With your tax sheltered investments and current bank accounts, you'll be able to maintain your present costs of living."

"Will you relay these figures to the staff?"

"Can do. I'll stress they're fortunate to be getting as much as they are."

"And what of you, Jim? I'm sorry it has come to this. How will you manage?"

Elmond managed a thin smile. "Something will turn up, it always does."

The news of Cassie's and Jim Elmond's engagement swept through the tramping group like a runaway brush fire. Gina Martin smiled knowingly. "Jim will know all the souks where you can ramp up your Visa card, fill your suitcase with the exotic perfumes of Araby, lucky woman." Her son in Vancouver berated her for latching onto a gold digger who would fleece her totally. Daughter Naomi Skyped her mother from an internet café in Lusaka and tearfully expressed her happiness at Cassie's new found romance.

Cassie herself was aware of a restless feeling to move out into the world. Now that the sale of Ballantrae was finalized, she felt an easy confidence in Jim's investment strategies to secure both their futures. Emotionally she felt a lingering unease about her physical desires inside this marriage. She tried not to think about separate beds, hoping they would in time forge a bond of intimacy.

The marriage left Cassie grateful and buoyant. She found new pleasure in cooking for two, and relaxed tableside chats. Absent were the hard, often unfounded, worries of a young bride. She looked ten years younger Gina Martin had said. Who would have guessed that marriage was better than a weekend spa treatment? Jim continued his volunteer work with the miniature railway. When he retreated to his lengthy solitudes with his computer, "to check the latest market indices", she busied herself with a good book or a brisk walk.

In the fall, after their return from a ten day walking trip in the Yorkshire Dales, Cassie began to think about the costs involved. Energized, she wondered could they afford more of these breaks over a year? With Jim's talk of futures, high risk funds, shorting, and capital gains, Cassie was at a loss to understand their exact financial standing. She determined to educate herself in this arcane science called Investment.

On a day when Jim was off to captain the miniature railway, Cassie went into his office to begin her financial education. She flipped open the top of his laptop computer, anxious to Google some of the more esoteric terms. To her surprise the screen burst into full display.

157

She frowned, amused and delighted at the images before her. The screen was full of compact shots of women in nursing garb, holding children of various ages toward the camera. Most were of African or Asian parentage. They showed in common gap-toothed smiles, or shy glances on their adult supporters. In one photograph a scrawny goat lounged in the doorway of a mud and wattle hut.

A curious lightness held her as she tried to unravel the meaning and depth of this montage. Momentarily she thought of her Naomi, labouring away in the heat of an African village, and was all her discomfort making any lasting difference in her students' lives? She puzzled over Jim's actions and motives. What were his contributions to these faraway causes?

Slowly she lowered the computer lid. She walked to the window. On the path beside the river a young boy was tossing a stick for his excited dog.

Jim sat back into the padding of the chair. "It's a mystery and disgrace in some poorer countries, why outside aid money often doesn't reach intended beneficiaries. Such as the orphaned children in those photos. International funds are stolen, misdirected, whatever. So I try to soften the injustice somewhat."

He stared into his wine glass; then he took a cautious sip. "It's where I go, overseas, in the hope of shaking some funds from local agencies, directing them to the kids in need. If they need medical care I try to circle local bureaucracies, get them urgent help." He studied her expression. "If it means paying *baksheesh* I consider it money well spent. Sometimes I'll get familiar with a paint brush, or a hammer. Those buildings always need a spot of repair. I wanted to tell you before we married. I should have, now I see that."

Though grateful that he offered her the truth of his trips abroad, she was struck with the personal horrors heaped among the array of photos, the risk of disease, injury, criminal attack. But that would not deter him. Years ago he had lifted her from disgrace and possible custody. Being the man he was he would continue to offer that solace to sufferers elsewhere. So the truth she owed him, that she had entered into an unspoken bargain in part to save him from unemployment, had he already guessed at?

They stood up and walked into the hallway, toward the bedroom. Not for a while would they discuss the real and present dangers in Jim's distant forays, choosing not to trespass into their mutual privacy. Instead, they spoke lightly of the forthcoming outing of the tramping club to Deckers Falls and the lovely patio luncheon at the inn there.

About the author
The author lives and writes in Ontario, where in his rec moments he riffs Beatles and blues on his Hohner harmonica, and reads widely – e.g. Ancient Greek tragedy, Norse sagas, medieval whodunnits. His flash and short fiction have appeared in various outlets.

The Litter

Jeanne Davies

Iris sat on the edge of her seat grasping hold of her phone. Her violet-blue eyes gazed down at Ebony who was lying with her head resting on Iris's foot. Iris stretched down to caress the Labrador's head, gently stroking the dog's black velveteen ears. Ebony's eyes slowly opened and stared soulfully back at her.

"I'm so sorry that you had to endure all those horrible tests, my baby," Iris whispered.

Dennis came in with a mug of tea.

"Any news?" he asked.

Iris raised her head sharply to look at her husband, her shoulder length auburn hair flicking up like tongues of fire. Recognising his wife's exasperated expression, Dennis retreated quickly to the kitchen.

At that moment the phone rang.

"I have good news for you Mrs. Turner," the voice on the phone said. "Ebony's hip and eye scores are perfect. From a vet's point of view there's no reason why you shouldn't go ahead with breeding from her; she's a very healthy dog. However, I would recommend that you contact her breeder when you've found a suitable mate to ensure their genealogy doesn't conflict in any way."

Iris wasn't convinced this good news was exactly what she wanted to hear. Unlike Dennis, she was worried that becoming a mother could change Ebony's lovely temperament. She had secretly hoped that her dog wouldn't be properly equipped to reproduce the pedigree Black Labrador puppies Dennis so badly desired.

"Well, that's fantastic news, isn't it Iris?" Dennis said, having been listening surreptitiously at the door. "Now we need to find a suitable "husband" for her," he chirped.

160

"But she's only a baby Dennis, my baby, and I'm not sure I want her to go through all this mating and giving birth thing," said Iris.

"She's two now, Iris, and the books say it is an optimum age for breeding as they're young and healthy. Anyway, we discussed this before; it fulfils her destiny, and we can have pick of the litter from the beautiful puppies she'll produce."

"But there are so many risks. If you were to be honest, it's all about the money with you, isn't it Dennis," Iris said angrily.

Immediately sensing a quarrel rising, Ebony lifted her head from Iris's foot and looked nervously at Dennis and then back at Iris. Her beautiful dark brown eyes were outlined in a light beige which made them stand out more than other black Labradors. She glared at the couple showing the whites of her eyes and blinked her eyelashes several times in panic. Iris immediately reassured Ebony and took her swiftly into the kitchen to have some carrot and broccoli sticks.

Dennis followed them, tentatively placing a reassuring arm around his wife's shoulders.

"You know we can't afford a holiday and it's been over five years since our last one. We both deserve it don't we, especially since your cancer scare?"

Iris softened. She looked into Dennis's jolly round face with his twinkling blue eyes and snub nose. She noticed his thinning fair hair, increasingly turning to silver and sparse on the top. He had supported her through so much and she had always felt guilty that she couldn't give him children of their own. She knew he meant well, but he didn't seem to have the same connection to Ebony that she did. She badly needed a holiday too, but only if they could find somewhere dog friendly for Ebony and her new pup.

The next day Dennis set the procedure in motion. He

had already researched the best stud dogs in the area and contacted a lady called Di, who seemed to know everything there was to know about Labrador mating and whelping. They arranged an appointment to look at her stud dogs.

Iris couldn't bear the thought of it all and decided to take Ebony out for a long walk instead of going along with Dennis. Every Tuesday she met up with Florence, her next-door neighbour, and her old dog, Freddie, who was eleven. They would walk for hours roaming across the beautiful nearby countryside. Fred was a Saint Bernard with a very calm and gentle nature, a real gentle giant. He found Ebony a bit boisterous at times but was always kind to her, often protecting her from other dogs; they often touched noses through a hole in the fence. Despite Ebony's attempts to play, Fred preferred to just plod along loyally beside his owner, thoughtfully observing her antics from a distance. Sometimes he just lay down nonchalantly to watch her spin and prance around him.

It was a beautiful spring day with a blue azure sky. There was a layer of thin ice over the pathways which made Ebony skid about excitedly at high speed. Fred looked enviously at her and just for a few moments skipped along beside her. They had always been friends, often barking messages across to each other at night when there were foxes about.

"Don't worry, Iris," said Florence. "Dennis is right that it is natural for them to have pups. I'm sure Ebony will be a wonderful mother and they say it can be good for a bitch to have one litter before she's spayed."

"But things can go wrong, can't they?" said Iris, her forehead rippling into a frown. "I've read some horrible stories on the internet about the mothers dying whilst giving birth and whole litters being born dead. I'm not sure I can cope, Flo."

"Just think, Iris, Ebony's mother survived it and how many puppies did she bring into this world?"

"Ten," said Iris reflectively.

"And my Fred's mum is still sprightly at the ripe old age of fourteen!"

As always, Florence was right. Ten years her senior, a widow who had grown up on her father's farm, she had more wisdom than anyone Iris ever knew. She told Iris that she helped her father deliver lambs in the spring and at one point the family had a total of fourteen cats and eight dogs, as well as hens and ducks in the yard.

"I'm only next door and I can be on call to help. You never know, I might even be tempted to buy a puppy from you... might perk old Fred up a bit."

Despite Flo's practical nature, Iris knew how she spoiled Freddie rotten. Every morning, he would be given a cup of tea (without sugar of course) followed by five small bone biscuits. She fed him the best food on the market and gave him many dietary additives to help keep his joints and coat healthy. Flo said that Fred had been her soul mate and best friend ever since he was eight weeks old; he'd got her through the worst of times, and the best of times in her life.

A few weeks later, Ebony was in the middle of her season, so Dennis drove her to the black Labrador stud dog he'd chosen and gained approval for from Ebony's breeder. Iris decided to go shopping in an attempt to distract herself from the reality of the situation. When they returned home, Iris was relieved to see that Ebony didn't appear to have been traumatised by her experience that day.

"Let's hope that was money well spent." Dennis sighed.

"Is that all you can think of?" said Iris. She scowled at Dennis, then continued to stir the bolognaise sauce for supper with great vigour.

163

"Well, it almost cost the price of a pup, Iris," he said. "He is a very handsome boy though and will make a good sire. She's due to visit him again in a few days' time, just to ensure the mating was a success."

The next morning Iris and Florence walked across the frosty fields together chatting about Ebony's health. A pair of buzzards were sweeping and turning their dark silhouettes against the silent blue sky and calling lamentedly to each other. It was a beautiful morning. Ebony loved the white frost and began rolling around in it excitedly. Fred decided to lie down in it and roll over on to his back. Suddenly both dogs bolted off after a rabbit and disappeared into a small area of woodland in the far corner of the field, causing a murder of crows to rise from the treetops squawking.

"Well, Fred's never caught a rabbit in his life," laughed Florence.

"Neither has Ebony, thankfully," said Iris.

The women continued walking and chatting but after a while they became aware that the dogs had been gone some while. Iris had been taking Ebony to training classes for over a year, so she blew her whistle hard several times. Eventually the dogs emerged from the copse. Fred was out of breath and Ebony had actually caught the rabbit. Iris was horrified but Florence persuaded the dog to drop it and they left it for some hungry fox to take home for his supper.

When Iris arrived home, she found Dennis building a whelping box for the puppies in the breakfast room.

"You'll never guess, Dennis, but Ebony caught a rabbit on the walk today!"

"Really, but just look at this Iris," Dennis said, proudly standing back to admire his workmanship. "There'll be plenty of space in there for Ebony and all her puppies."

Iris peered suspiciously inside the huge oblong box.

"They'll be safe in there from any dangers," added

Dennis. "And we can put in some of that vet bed lining that's easy to clean."

Despite her lack of enthusiasm, as weeks went by Iris was beginning to get quite excited; she was even choosing names like Jet for their new puppy. She'd noticed Ebony seemed more tired than usual and was uncharacteristically grumpy. She went off her food, so Iris bought some expensive prescription brand from the vet together with some pregnancy vitamins. Before long, her belly began to grow daily at a rapid rate. They decided to take her to the vet for a scan.

"Congratulations, Ebony has a minimum of seven puppies inside her and everything looks good," the vet told them. "In fact, looking at the size of her, there could even be a few more!"

As soon as they returned home, Ebony flopped on the sofa with a big sigh.

"Do you think she's going to be alright, Dennis?" Iris said worriedly.

"Of course she is! This calls for a celebratory drink," Dennis said doing a little jig on the spot.

He removed a bottle of champagne from the fridge but before he could pop the cork, Ebony started panting heavily in the sitting room. Iris rushed to her and there on the sofa was what looked like a shiny, silky bag. She could just see inside a little puppy wrapped up in a gossamer cocoon.

"Quick Dennis, go and get Florence… we are going to need her help," Iris said in a panic.

When Florence arrived, Ebony was gently cleaning her new pup whilst also giving birth to another, on the sofa. Florence carefully delivered another four puppies in the whelping box whilst Iris climbed inside the box and cuddled and reassured the new mother. By the time the eighth puppy was delivered, Dennis began to look very puzzled. He leaned over the side of the whelping box and shook his head.

"Do they look like a funny colour to you?" Dennis asked.

Both women stopped in their tracks. The beautiful little puppies were not the same glossy black colour as Ebony, nor were they the colour of the stud dog Dennis had found. Each puppy had brown and white markings

"They are much larger than any new-born Labrador puppies I've ever seen," said Florence thoughtfully.

"But they will be okay, won't they Florence?" asked Iris.

"Oh yes, they look heathy enough," she replied. "But I think that you are both the proud grandparents of eight beautiful Labernard puppies!"

"What do you mean?" Dennis said.

"It seems that my old Fred and Ebony have been better friends than any of us imagined," Florence said with a grin. "The old rascal!"

The Labernard is a patient, friendly and affectionate dog much like the parent breeds that create him – the outgoing Labrador Retriever and gentle giant Saint Bernard – both bred as working dogs. They are large to giant sized dogs that need a firm hand because they can be quite wilful so training is best started young. Common colours are white, yellow, brown, tan, black and red while their coats are short and dense, with a thick double-coat which can make them battle in the heat. They shed moderately so will need regular brushing to keep their coats healthy. The Labernard will need a lot of exercise so will be best suited to an active family who enjoy taking him out on excursions.

This story is dedicated to Fred, Chocolate Labrador, who died this year.

About the author
Jeanne Davies has always enjoyed making up stories and visiting other people's worlds and feelings. She began to submit to competitions a few years back and has had many short stories, flash fiction and poetry included in anthologies and magazines in the UK and USA. Most recently her story "Bognor Mermaid" has been published in the anthology *Folklore* by the Amphibian Literary Society Press. Her first single author anthology *Drawn by the Sea* was published by Bridge House in 2020.

The Pursuit

Michael Noonan

It was 16 March. I, Karl Hoffmann, had journeyed from Asunción in a second-hand car I'd purchased there, to the small, provincial Paraguayan town of Valdez. It was a hot sticky day and I wore a wide brimmed hat, and sunglasses, to keep the merciless brightness of the tropical sun from my eyes.

When I eventually reached the outskirts of the town a feeling of deep unease and foreboding overcame me, which, like the incessant heat, I couldn't shake off.

It had been a long and taxing journey to Valdez. I had stalked my prey across half a dozen Central and South American countries over the previous eighteen months. In places as geographically diverse as La Paz, Buenos Aires, Mexico City, Tegucigalpa, Valparaiso and Quito, I had sought to apprehend him, but the man had cunningly eluded me on each occasion, as if some mysterious sixth sense had kept him informed of the approach of danger.

In an envelope, in an inside pocket, I had a photograph of that same individual. An affable, well dressed, healthy looking man in his early seventies, with an easy smile and vivid blue eyes. The last person one could imagine to be a war criminal with the blood of thousands on his hands.

Max Kesselmann had been born into a prosperous, middle-class household in Dortmund, Germany. He was the only surviving child of the family, a twin brother having died in tragic circumstances in his late teens.

At any other period he would in all probability have pursued a comfortable bourgeois career, like his parents, but on leaving university was instead seduced by the heady rhetoric, the drums, marches and banners of the

National Socialist Party. Much to the disgust of his liberal-minded parents he joined the SS, Hitler's black-uniformed guards.

An intelligent, though thoroughly amoral individual, he rose rapidly up the ranks of that grisly organisation, receiving a full indoctrination along the way, and after War broke out was put in charge of an Einsatzgruppen death squad, whose special purpose was the extermination of Jews and other so called racial sub-groupings, behind the lines, on the vast tracts of territory newly plundered by the advancing Wehrmacht, on the Eastern Front, following the invasion of Soviet Russia.

Of course there were other Nazi war criminals to pursue at that time, with even darker records of inhumanity to their names. But there was a personal animus behind my endeavour to track down this particular individual. One of Kesselmann's many victims had been my brother, Anton. He had fled Germany, months after the Nazis came to power, to Lithuania, where he had relations – as he had fears and misgivings about Hitler's new Reich. Yet it was only a temporary respite he had bought. For when the Nazis pushed eastwards, in Operation Barbarossa, he, along with thousands of others, was tracked down by those special units whose task wasn't warfare, but racial genocide.

It was in the dragnet of one such unit, under Kesselmann's command, that he was caught. Within days, he, and several hundred others, were compelled to dig a vast trench in some open country outside of Vilnius. They were shot in the back of the head and pushed into that same trench, which was then covered over with soil. The unit, under its eager young commander, went onto cleanse further areas of their non-Ayran populations.

I myself, also sensing what was to come, had left Germany in 1933, for the safer haven of Britain, and then the United States, where I became a university student, and so avoided the fate that befell so many of my compatriots. However I kept a keen interest in the fate of my family and friends, during those dark and tumultuous times.

Though having been suspected of escaping his homeland, via one of the infamous ratlines, as the Nazi state crumbled to rubble, Kesselmann had yet been unaccounted for since the end of the War. It hadn't been known if he was alive or dead. Then there were sightings of a person who resembled Kesselmann; in Bolivia, then in Ecuador, and then in Chile. And I was convinced, despite the doubts that others expressed, that Kesselmann was still alive and residing, incognito, somewhere in the great landmass of Latin America.

Then a journalist, who had resided for some years in Chile – as the foreign correspondent for a respected newspaper, and who was sympathetic to my cause – was informed by a contact that someone who bore a distinct resemblance to Kesselmann was living in a quiet suburb of Valparaiso and that he was, purportedly, a Swiss businessman, who went by the name of Andreas Schell. He immediately passed the information onto me, and it was then that my single-minded and almost obsessional quest to track down and bring to justice that notorious war criminal, began.

I had sent a team of trusted confederates over to Valparaiso to keep a discreet watch over that mysterious individual. Photos were taken, by hidden cameras; and intensive background checks were made. And within a matter of months it was established that the alleged Swiss businessman was indeed the Nazi war criminal, Max Kesselmann.

It seemed that my quest was about to reach fruition. A case was almost ready to be lodged with the authorities, for the apprehension, and extradition of Kesselmann, in order that he could stand trial for crimes against humanity. Yet by that time Kesselmann himself – either through suspicions, or a tip off – felt that things weren't entirely safe for him in the city that had been his home. With ruthless dispatch he sold his business, and his comfortable suburban home – abruptly terminated the few relationships and friendships he had made, particularly with the expat German-speaking community – and hurriedly left the city for safer sanctuary elsewhere. And so the task of seeking to track him down, and bring him to justice, began all over again.

For months Kesselmann was nowhere to be seen. Then there were fleeting sightings of him in other cities and towns of Latin America. I would make haste to any destination where it was thought he might be holed up. But Kesselmann always seemed to be a step ahead of me and my associates, and would disappear again as soon as I arrived on the scene. It was like chasing a spectre. Then there was a lengthy dearth of even those fleeting sightings of him. The trail had gone cold. Kesselmann had slipped off the radar screen, and no one knew where he was. Though I had a number of dedicated assistants scouring the continent for any sight of the criminal.

Then, after months of demoralising quietude, solid information arrived that told me where I could find my quarry, without the prospect of him slyly slipping away before I arrived on the scene. It was the obscure little known town of Valdez, deep in the Paraguayan interior. Yet what made Valdez so strikingly different from all the other destinations where I had sought to corner the elusive Kesselmann, was that I had actually been invited there by Kesselmann himself.

While in my hotel room in Lima, at work on my papers, I received a letter. It went as follows:

Dear Mr Hoffmann,

I know well that you have been seeking to track me down for over a year now. I also know what motivates you in this singular quest, Mr Hoffmann, and why you wish to seek me out. I have grown tired of this life on the run that you and your confederates have forced me to lead, at home nowhere, without being able to settle in any one place, never secure, or at peace, and always wondering when vengeance will catch up with me. I am an old man, and perhaps not quite the monster you envisage me as being, Mr Hoffmann. The things that concern you happened so long ago, in a period of war and upheaval, where millions of people died, and not just those of your race, and where normal standards and values didn't apply. Aside from which, as you must well know, I was merely a cog in the machine, an apparatchik, to use that old Soviet term. Obeying the orders of my superiors, in a military command structure, and within a totalitarian system, where obedience was of the essence and where the questioning of orders was forbidden. Indeed, anyone foolish enough to do so would be deemed a traitor to the party and the fatherland, and would in effect be signing his own death warrant.

I am writing to inform you that I have been living in the small provincial town of Valdez, in Paraguay, for some weeks now, and intend to stay put for some time to come. You are welcome to come here, Mr Hoffmann. Perhaps we can discuss things, of mutual concern, in a quiet and civilised manner. Despite my reputation, you will find that I am quite a congenial person. I have neither horns nor a tail, despite all the things that are written about me in the newspapers and am very much a mere human, as you are. You're

welcome to come at any time. Valdez is a small,
provincial town, so you should find me quite easily. I
look forward to seeing you, at some time.

Yours sincerely
Max Kesselmann.

I was perplexed and puzzled by the contents of the letter.
Was it a trick? Was he in Valdez at all? And if so, did he
intend to turn the tables on me, and lure me, the hunter, into
a trap, in that small, isolated, provincial town? Did he want
to try to bribe me into giving up the chase? It was alleged
that he was a man of considerable means. Or did he
genuinely wish for a meeting, to discuss things with me,
relating to his past, in the open? Perhaps even a mass
murderer, in the twilight of his years, might have a change
of heart, and might wish to express guilt and remorse for
what he had done?

It was with some reluctance that I left for Asunción and
then Valdez itself. Though, in order to placate my growing
doubts and suspicions I came armed with a fully loaded gun
and spare ammunition.

The town was a mixture of crumbling old buildings, some
dating to colonial times, and rather gimcrack modern
structures, where the pace of life was so casual and
unhurried it almost seemed to take place in slow motion.
Old men, many with inscrutable, weather-beaten, Indian
faces, and large wide hats on their heads, sat – either lazily
talking to each other, or in self-contained silence – at street
cafes or on benches, under shady, arcaded walkways. On
the rutted, potholed roads, horse and oxen-pulled vehicles
seemed to outnumber the motorised traffic.

After booking a room, under an alias, on the fourth floor
of the town's one half-decent hotel, I walked down the main
street. Under the ceaseless sticky heat, sweat oozed from

my limbs and torso. I waved the incessant flies away from below the brim of my hat. I stopped a passer-by; a tall, silver-haired man – hastily showed him the photograph of Kesselmann and asked, in Spanish, if he'd ever seen that particular individual.

The man studied the photograph. "I don't know." He looked with a marked undercurrent of suspicion, at the well-heeled interloper from the outside world.

I smiled wryly and nodded my head. Why shouldn't an impoverished local use any available and legitimate opportunity for some extra remuneration? I would surely have done the same in his position.

I took two crisp notes from my wallet and handed them to the local, who looked down at them with wide, unblinking eyes. He swiftly pocketed them, thanked me profusely and his memory suddenly revitalized by that transaction, he pointed an arm down the flyblown street.

"There's a cantina at the end of the street. He goes there every evening around seven and sits at a table."

"Thanks. You've been a great help."

"Thank you, señor," he replied.

Just after seven I tentatively entered the cantina. And sure enough, sat at a table, smoking a pipe – a bottle of wine and a half filled glass before him – was Kesselmann. Though he didn't look nearly as jovial, clean cut and well dressed, as in the photo. Indeed he seemed almost like a local peasant, with his slovenly attire and unshaven face. Was this all an act and a performance, I wondered to myself, in order to try and fit into his new environment and draw attention away from his true identity and his criminal past.

I slowly made my way over and, despite the beating of my heart and the shaking of my hands, I glowered down at the man I had tracked and pursued for so many months.

"Max Kesselmann. It's taken a long time to catch up with you."

The German looked up at me with alarm and fear in his eyes.

"What are you talking about? I'm not Max Kesselmann!" he insisted vehemently, as the few customers and proprietor looked on in inquisitive silence.

"But I have your letter. You---"

In a state of great agitation the man got to his feet. He picked up his ragged hat, knocked the embers of his pipe into an ashtray, then spilled some coins onto the table top. "I've done nothing. I'm not a war criminal. I've nothing to be ashamed of. You must leave me alone. D'you hear?" He stared at me with anger as well as fear.

I was scathing in my contempt for that performance. "So you're trying to deny it all now. It never happened. After inviting me all the way over here to Valdez. All those thousands you and your comrades murdered on the Eastern Front. Well that won't wash Mr Kesselmann. We have the facts. We have the evidence."

"Leave me alone," he all but screamed, as he ran past the wide-eyed customers and the shocked proprietor, out of the cantina and along the road to the outskirts of the town.

I made haste back to my car, parked in a forecourt of the hotel, drove off in the direction of the cantina, then followed the route Kesselmann had taken out of the town. And I wondered to myself all the while, in my growing confusion, why Kesselmann had sent me such an emollient letter, and then acted in such a querulous, prickly and frightened manner, when I had approached him? Or did he have a sudden change of heart at the prospect of opening the nightmare horror of his previous life and being brought to account for his frightful crimes?

After ten minutes I came across the bedraggled

Kesselmann, walking hastily by the side of a country road, with bleak shrub-land on either side. He was a far cry from the arrogant, uniformed Nazi killer on the Eastern Front. I slowed the car to a walking speed and wound down the window.

"Well the boot's on the other foot now, Mr Kesselmann. You hunted our people down in their thousands and murdered them without mercy. Now it's your turn to be hunted down, and brought to justice."

Kesselmann turned his haunted face towards me. "I'm not Max Kesselmann. I've killed none of your people. I wasn't even there when it happened. I'm an innocent man. Why don't you get out of Valdez and just leave me in peace?"

"Still trying to deny it all."

"I've done nothing. And I'm not the one you're looking for."

"You've managed to evade justice, all these years. But you're going to pay for your crimes."

I parked the car by a verge of the road, got out and followed the man on foot.

Kesselmann, having gone beyond words to express himself, took out an ancient revolver from an inside pocket and pointed it with tremulous hand, at me. "I warned you to leave me alone. But you wouldn't listen."

"What the hell are you doing?" I shouted.

A shot just winged past my right ear. I ran back, and crouched behind my car, as another shot pierced the air. In desperation I retrieved my own gun, and as Kesselmann approached, intent on killing me, I tried to aim to merely wound or incapacitate, just as they do in cop movies and westerns, but I wasn't a good shot and was too nervous and jumpy to steady myself. The old man was hit through the heart: he gasped, crumpled and fell, dead to the ground.

I hadn't wanted such an abrupt and sudden conclusion to my search for Kesselmann. It was too clean and quick an end for such a monster. I would have preferred it, had he been arrested, stood trial, faced cross-examination, the testimony of witnesses and the few surviving victims of his handiwork, then a guilty sentence and a lonely prison cell for the rest of his life. Also, I hadn't been able to tell him, to his face, that he had killed my brother.

Now it would be me who would face a jail sentence, or even a death sentence, if the nature of that killing ever came to light. Fortunately it was a quiet road and no traffic was about. The only eyes to see were those of birds and some nearby sheep that had been roused from their grazing. I pulled the body over a hedge and placed it in a ditch, which I covered with soil, branches, stones and pieces of wood, till it was completely obscured from sight. No doubt it would be discovered in time; but by then I hoped I would be safely out of the country.

I drove back to town. It was evening and the sleepy town was enjoying what little nightlife it aspired to. I swiftly made my way to my hotel room.

I poured myself a stiff drink to try and steady my nerves, swallowed half of it, left the glass on a table and hastily set about packing my belongings into a travelling bag. I took the bag down to the car and locked it in the boot. I went back to the hotel room for the last time, to check that I hadn't left any incriminating material about. I entered the room, picked up my glass and took a sip, then suddenly froze, as I realised that the door had been left slightly ajar, when I distinctly remembered shutting it as I left to put the case in the car. I looked around the room and noticed that the door to the balcony was also open and a balmy night breeze issued into the room.

I also saw, with an almost nauseous feeling of dread,

that a distinct form stood on the balcony, watching me, impassively. I daren't move. I stood, with glass in hand, not knowing what to do, or what was happening. The moment stretched agonizingly, with only the ticking of a clock, the warm, lapping breeze, and my own heartbeat, to penetrate the appalling silence.

The shadowy form took on motion, and slowly entered the room. A tall, dapper man emerged into view. He wore a well-cut suit, shiny black shoes, and there was a stylish felt hat on his head, with a feather in its side, just as on some of the photographs I had seen. He wore a pair of dark glasses and a gun in his right hand was pointed directly at me.

"We meet at long last, Mr Hoffmann. I've looked forward to this day for some time now."

The stranger removed his sunglasses, folded them, and slid them into his top pocket. I looked on in open disbelief. He was the very incarnation of Kesselmann. The living duplicate of the man I had shot and killed that very day. Though this figure was a more elegant, confident apparition altogether.

"May I introduce myself. I'm Max Kesselmann."

"You can't be Kesselmann. He's dead. I shot him this evening."

"You shot my brother, Heinz. My identical twin brother."

I shook my head. "But your brother died back in the Twenties. It's on the record."

"That's what the authorities think, Mr Hoffmann. Perhaps I should tell you the full story. My brother killed a man in a brawl, in a beer cellar, after they had argued with each other." He smiled, bleakly. "And like many arguments at that time, it was all about politics. But he managed to escape before the police arrived. My family and I didn't want to see my brother tried and hanged, so we arranged for a little accident to happen. We flung his jacket, with his papers, his wallet and a small photograph of himself, into a lake. I alerted the police and when they found his jacket, and the identifying material it contained, it was assumed that he had either died in a boating accident or killed himself. The case was closed. At the same time, using some influential family connections, we managed to obtain some new documents for my brother. And with the aid of a new name and identity, we smuggled him out of Germany. He knew that he could never return to his homeland again, and he went all the way to Paraguay. He spent the first twenty years in Asunción, where, with the money we supplied him, he managed to establish a new life for himself. And then he moved here, to Valdez, where he set himself up as a small farmer."

"So I killed your brother?"

"Indeed." Kesselmann smiled. "Just as I killed yours, all those years ago. Yes, I've done my research on you as well, Mr Hoffmann. At least on that score we're now even."

"Why did you write to ask me to come here, Mr Kesselmann? To Valdez?"

"I was sick of being the prey, the hunted one, Mr Hoffmann. It goes against all my instincts. So I decided to turn the tables on you. I invited you over to Valdez, precisely because my twin brother lives, or rather lived, here. I may have saved his life back in the Twenties, but my brother and I never saw eye to eye on politics. He was a committed communist. While my beliefs, of course, were the polar opposite. And from the day I joined the National Socialist Party, we have had no contact with each other." He smiled again. "Until recently that is. He wanted nothing to do with me, and like yourself, detested everything I stood for. He was resigned to living his anonymous, almost peasant life, as long as he could distance himself as far as possible from all

179

connection with his twin brother. And so imagine his horror and disgust, when, after all those years, I contacted Heinz, and informed him that the famous Nazi-hunter, Karl Hoffmann, was shortly to arrive in Valdez, with the mistaken notion that he, Heinz, was the war criminal, Max Kesselmann. I knew that it would drive my brother to the brink of madness and that as such, he would be capable of the most desperate and irrational behaviour."

"So the letter was just a trick."

"It certainly served its purpose Mr Hoffmann. If you were to kill my brother, or he was to kill you, I would find myself in a much more agreeable situation. If he killed you, I would be free of my greatest tormentor. If however, you killed him, as is now the case, there could also be positive consequences for me. Seeing that he is of German origin and physically identical to me, it would be rapidly concluded that this was indeed the notorious war criminal, Max Kesselman, who had assumed another persona, and had adopted an invented name, and had lived an obscure life in the interior of Paraguay, in order to hide and conceal his true identity, just as Eichmann, Mengele and others had done. And many would regard his death as being the work of Mossad agents. The case would be closed and I would be free to resume my existence as a blameless Swiss expatriate."

"What d'you intend to do now?"

"Of the two options, my brother killing you, or you killing my brother, I would have much preferred the former. You're a resourceful and intelligent man. I feel that you would have suspected that something was amiss, and dug deeper into my brother's background. You are after all a professional investigator. You may well have found out that the man you killed was another person entirely. And then it would be back to square one."

"So you intend to kill me too!"

"I'm afraid that it has to come to this, Mr Hoffmann. I will never be safe and secure while you are still alive."

I looked down at the black gun muzzle of the luger and a bitter smile came to my lips. "Well it won't be the first time, will it?"

"No, but it should be the last." He smiled, with the apparition of good humour. "And then I can go back to resume my quiet existence, with my adopted identity that I have become quite comfortable with. Though this time I shall take up permanent residence in Asunción."

"And you think you'll get away with it?"

"I don't see why not. Indeed, until you and your associates appeared on the scene, my life was quite secure on this continent. And I would point out, Mr Hoffmann, that Paraguay isn't exactly a liberal, Western democracy. And its leader, General Stroessner, a man of German extraction I should add, has always been quite sympathetic to expatriates, of my nature. But, we've talked long enough, Mr Hoffmann. Our little meeting must come to an end. To tell you the truth, I wish that things had never come this far, or that my brother had had to be involved in this regrettable business. But you've made this a question of my survival, or yours."

He leant over and with his free hand switched on the radio that stood on an adjacent table. An anonymous pop track blared through the speaker. He turned up the volume till the sound was loud enough to cover the noise of a gunshot.

In an act of spontaneous impulse, as Kesselmann straightened himself, to re-aim his gun, I flung the contents of my drink into Kesselmann's eyes. He shrieked and shook his head, as I leapt across and pushed the man backwards. We fell into the balcony, upending the table and sending the radio crashing onto the floor in the process. I managed in the struggle to push Hoffmann aside. He clambered to his feet and with fear and panic jumped backwards to avoid further entanglement with his pursuer, and to find some space from which to shoot and kill me. But in his haste and impatience he went too far and too fast to be contained safely within the narrow confines of the balcony, and his body, carried away by its own momentum, crashed against and then over the parapet. He waved his arms helplessly, shrieked a wild curse in his mother tongue, and fell, for what seemed an interminable time, until he collided with the stone paving below.

Birds squawked and took wing into the black, clammy, tropical night. There were screams from some passers-by. Running steps were heard in the dark spaces below. Lights flickered on behind various windows, and blinds were opened.

In the gathering confusion I switched off the radio, ran from the room, down the steps, out of the hotel and into my waiting car. I drove, at full speed, towards Asunción.

It was with a sense of profound relief that I took a flight, from the Paraguayan capital, to Lima. I later found out that Max Kesselmann had died as a result of that fall.

About the author
Michael Noonan lives in Halifax (home of the Piece Hall), Yorkshire. Has a background in food production, retail and office work. Has had stories, articles and artworks published in literary magazines and anthologies, in the US, UK and Europe. A volume of his stories, *Seven Tall Tales*, is available at Amazon, as a book or kindle. His comic play *A Restive Audience*, has been published in *Hello Godot! An Anthology of one act plays Volume 2* by Freshwords publishing, in the US, and his play *The Conference Speech*, has been published by the same company.
@readyverbiage
https://www.behance.net/gallery/182795873/Imaginative-Images

The Silver Card

Seth Pilevsky

"Welcome to GarMart," Eddie said with as much enthusiasm as he could muster, which wasn't all that much.

An old woman with large brown hearing aids and a few grey hairs on her chin stepped in front of the register.

The conveyor belt brought Eddie a bottle of prune juice, three oranges, one large grapefruit, unsalted walnuts and instant oatmeal.

"Sixteen dollars and twelve cents," he droned after he scanned the items.

She looked up at him with milky-blue eyes. "I have a coupon."

Eddie took the coupon. It was for 10% off of the prune juice.

"Sorry lady, it's expired."

"What?"

"It's expired," he repeated, louder.

"No, I don't think it is. Can you look at the date?"

The checkout line started to grow behind the old woman.

"I did. It's expired."

"It can't be."

"Lady, pay for your items or move along. Other people are waiting."

A tall and thin man with a buzz cut and a name tag that said Tracey walked up behind Eddie. "Is there a problem?" he asked, looking down at Eddie. Eddie was as short as Tracey was tall. He felt Tracey's eyes on the top of his head.

"Yes, I have a coupon," the old lady said, "and this young man is being very rude."

"I was not being rude," said Eddie.

"Eddie," warned Tracey.

"I didn't do anything wrong," Eddie said to Tracey.

"Ma'am," said Tracey. "Please come off the line. I'll help you out with your coupon."

The old woman and Tracy walked over to the manager's counter.

Eddie called for the next customer.

Pedro, in the register next to Eddie, shook his head.

"You're going to pay for that later, my friend."

Without turning around, Eddie responded. "Pay for what? I was totally professional. Polite even."

"You know what Loretta says about being polite?" Pedro asked.

Eddie rolled his eyes. "Pedro, in the two years that we've been working together, I don't think you've ever let a day go by without quoting your wife."

That elicited a belly laugh from Pedro.

"True enough. You know why?"

"Because you don't have your own opinions?"

"Very funny. No, it's because she's the smartest person I know."

"Maybe you don't know enough people."

"Don't bad-mouth my girl, Eddie," said Pedro, his ample moustache frowning over his lips. "I'd be nothing without my Loretta."

"Take it easy, man. I'm just messing with you. Tell me what Loretta says about being polite."

Pedro brightened. He took someone's credit card and ran it.

"*If you're polite, you'll be alright*," he said.

"That's terrible," said Eddie, bagging some heads of lettuce. "Just because it rhymes doesn't mean it's profound."

"Eddie," said Pedro. "You have a bad attitude."

"You have a bad attitude, Eddie," said Tracey, after the last customer left the store. The store was empty except for Tracey and Eddie. They were sitting across from each other in Tracey's office in the back of the supermarket.

"I'm sorry."

"I truly believe that you are," he said. "But this is not the first, second or third complaint we've gotten about you. You're short-tempered with the customers."

"Tracey, I run the express line. Ten items or less. People are always rushing me or trying to sneak in a full cart. Old people give me expired coupons. I deal with this stuff every day. If you moved me to a regular aisle, I wouldn't be having these problems."

"Eddie, it's not about the checkout counter. It's about you. You're constantly getting into it with customers. I'm afraid I'll have to let you go."

"Seriously?" Eddie asked, his dark eyes glaring at Tracey.

"Yes, I'm sorry."

"You can go to hell," Eddie said, as he untied his apron and threw it on the floor.

He stormed out of the front door of the restaurant into the parking lot. He was about to step into his car when he noticed something shiny on the ground, reflecting light from an outdoor pole lamp.

He picked it up. It was a silver card. On one side was an engraved image. It was the face of a skeleton with only one large eyeball, like a cyclops. Its jaw was set in an angry scowl. Eddie flipped over the card and read the inscription:

It was wise to pick me up.

I will shield you from bad luck.
If bad luck should come today,
turn my eye another way.
Whomever my eye shall see,
will have your luck and you'll be free!

Eddie examined the card. It looked like real silver, tarnished in the way silver gets when it's not polished.

"Hey Eddie, it's not personal," he heard Tracey say as he walked out of the supermarket towards his own car.

Eddie looked at the card and flashed the skeleton with the large eye and angry grimace towards Tracey.

A car pulled into the parking lot. Rhonda Garcia, the owner of the supermarket, got out of a red sports car. Eddie recognized her from her periodic visits to the GarMart. She looked angry.

"Ms. Garcia," Tracey said. "Nice to see you. What are you doing here so late? Is everything alright?"

"No, Tracey, everything is not alright. My bookkeeper can't reconcile the accounts for the store. You're stealing from me."

"No! I would never," he said, one hand on his heart.

"I don't believe you, you're fired."

"What?"

"You heard me," she said and then turned to face Eddie. "Who are you? Do you work for me?"

"I'm Eddie. I did work for you, but I was just fired by Tracey."

"You're rehired. Follow Tracey inside while he packs up his stuff. Make sure he doesn't take anything." She tossed a set of keys to Eddie. He caught them with one hand. "Then lock up the store."

Garcia got in her car and drove off.

Tracey walked back into the store to pack up his personal items.

Eddie kissed the silver card, still in his hand, placed it in his wallet, and followed his former boss into the supermarket.

"Say hi to your new boss," Pedro said, when Eddie walked into work the next day.

"You were promoted?" he asked. Why was Pedro promoted over him, he wondered. Eddie had seniority. He was working at the GarMart for five years. Pedro was hired only two years ago. Maybe it was his age? Pedro was pushing sixty and Eddie was still in his twenties. The unfairness of being passed over rankled Eddie.

"Yeah, Ms. Garcia called me last night after she fired Tracey. I can't believe he was stealing. She said that you were there. You have the keys?"

Eddie pulled them out of his pocket and handed them to Pedro.

"Thanks, now sweep the aisles!"

Eddie bristled. "That's not my job."

Pedro slapped him on the arm and laughed. "I was just teasing you, my friend. You gotta have a sense of humour. You know what Loretta says about teasing?"

Eddie bit back his reply and said, instead, to his new boss, "No, what does Loretta say about teasing?"

"*Be at ease with a little tease.*"

"Nice one," said Eddie, choking on his words.

"Right? Puts things into perspective. We all take ourselves too seriously."

Eddie put on his GarMart apron and got behind his aisle. The store had opened and customers were starting to trickle in.

A little after his lunch break, Eddie noticed his least favourite customer step onto his line. The old woman that got him fired fell into place behind a teenage girl with pink

187

hair and three earrings on each ear. The old woman had a red basket with some sort of pain cream, a bag of clementines and a jar of chocolate chip cookies. She had several yellowed strips of paper in her basket that looked like old coupons. There were only two people in front of her. The last thing that Eddie wanted was to spar with this woman, again, over her expired coupons. He looked at the other checkout lines. Each one was much longer than his. Eddie's line was the only express one and the old woman was almost up.

Suddenly, a crazy idea occurred to him. He dug into his pocket and pulled the silver card out of his wallet. He turned the etching of the angry skeleton face towards the Trinity. Trinity was two aisles away.

The old woman with the coupons blinked twice, left Eddie's line, and went to the back of Trinity's line, the longest line in the store.

A grin broke out on Eddie's face.

At the end of his shift, Eddie decided to test his silver card on something bigger than a grouchy old lady. He went to Daze, a nightclub that he and his girlfriend Carter liked to hang out at. The music pulsated so loud that he could hear it a block away. A balding bouncer, standing guard at the door with his arms folded, took one look at him and turned his head from side to side. No entry. Daze tried to balance the single men and women in the club at one time. Eddie could wait until he was allowed in, or he could try something else.

Eddie took his card out and turned the skeletal eye towards a young couple that was approaching the club.

"Sorry," the bouncer said to the couple. "We're full." Then he looked at Eddie and jutted his thumb towards the door to the club.

Eddie walked in. He met Carter at a club just like Daze a few months earlier. She was a professional dancer and knew her way around all the clubs in town.

Eddie believed that his silver card was the real thing, but he had one more test in mind before he was completely convinced. He scoured the club for the most unattainable girl he could find. A tall red-haired girl with blue eyes was sitting next to a man, in a booth. The man appeared to be her boyfriend. They were both impeccably dressed. Good. The man was taller, better looking and much stronger than Eddie. If this didn't work, then Eddie would likely not walk away unscathed.

"Hey," he said to the girl. "Wanna dance?"

"Walk. Away," the man told him, putting his arm around the girl. "While you still can."

"You heard him," the girl said, narrowing her eyes and spearing him with a dirty look.

Eddie took out his silver card and aimed the skeletal eye squarely at the man.

"Just kidding," said the girl, breaking out in a smile. "I would love to dance with you."

"Jean, are you messing with me?" the man asked.

"Lay off, Troy" she said to him, as she approached Eddie. "I wanna dance with this guy."

The man got up from the booth, clenched a fist and took a step in Eddie's direction. Eddie acted quickly. He turned the silver eye towards a man walking by the booth with two drinks in his hand. Troy pivoted and hit the man in the face. The drinks fell to the ground and the glasses shattered. Once the man got up, he threw himself at Troy and the fists started flying.

Eddie and Jean danced together while the fight he started spread around the nightclub. Once the dance was over, Eddie slipped out of Daze and went home, satisfied with the chaos he'd created and confident that anything he wanted was his for the taking.

Eddie went to work in the morning and started making plans. He would use the silver card to get Pedro's job. Pedro would be right back at the checkout counter where he belonged. His mind was swimming with the possibilities.

Right before lunchtime, his phone rang. It was Carter. He put on his wireless earbuds and answered the phone so he could scan and talk at the same time.

"Hey babe," he said. "What's up?"

"Don't *hey babe* me."

"What? Did I do something?"

"You were at Daze last night. Don't bother denying it. Jazz saw you dancing with another girl."

Eddie forgot that Carter had eyes and ears at Daze.

"It wasn't me."

"She took a picture with her phone."

A picture of Eddie and Jean hit his text messages.

"Okay, it was me, but it's not what you think. I can explain."

"Don't bother, Eddie. I think you just did me a huge favour. We're done."

She hung up the phone.

Pedro strode up to Eddie from his manager's station.

"Hey, no personal calls during your shift, man."

"Shut up, Pedro. Carter just broke up with me."

Pedro's eyes softened. "I'm sorry to hear that, man. I really am. Y'know what Loretta says about breakups? *Breakups may be rough, but they'll make you tough.* I truly believe that, Eddie. You may not want to hear it now, but you'll be alright."

Eddie felt his skin burn. He just lost his girlfriend. Carter dumped him! And Pedro had the nerve to serve up one of Loretta's idiotic platitudes? Now of all times? Who did he think he was? Before he could stop himself, he pulled out the silver card and turned the angry skeletal face towards Pedro.

"What is that?" Pedro asked.

Just then, his cellphone rang. Pedro walked up to the manager's booth to take the call.

Oh no, thought Eddie staring at the card. I take it back. I take it back. Please take it back.

He watched Pedro take the call. Even though he couldn't hear Pedro over the buzz of the customers, he knew that Loretta had called him and what she was saying to him. It was like watching a train as it was about to derail. Pedro's face went white. He looked very upset and spoke very quickly, urgently.

Eddie's phone pinged with a text. It was from Carter. He dropped the silver card in his apron's breast pocket.

"Giving you one more chance, Eddie. Don't make me regret it."

The winds of Eddie's luck shifted again. It didn't make him feel better, though. Eddie didn't even like Carter that much. Loretta was everything to Pedro. Even from a distance, he could see tears streaming down Pedro's cheeks. Pedro's hands shook and he dropped his phone on the ground. Pedro walked to the back of the store, his head down.

I can fix this, thought Eddie. I just need to get Loretta and Pedro in the store together. I'll push their bad luck onto a customer and get them back together.

Eddie's thoughts were interrupted by the sound of a loud thud coming from the front parking lot. The customers and employees ran out of the store to see what was going on. Eddie's heart thundered as he tried to squeeze his way through the crowd to get outside. He heard a woman scream ahead of him.

191

"Out of my way! Out of my way!" he shouted as he pushed through to the front of the crowd.

Eddie stared at a grey sedan. The top of the car was caved in. There was a body on it. It was Pedro, on his back. Eddie looked at the roof and realized that Pedro must have taken the back stairs to the roof and jumped. Tears formed in Eddie's eyes as he climbed onto the car and kneeled over Pedro's broken body.

Pedro's arms and legs were twisted in unnatural positions. Blood was seeping out of his mouth, coating his teeth and soaking his thick moustache. His eyes were open, blinking slowly. He was wheezing as the life force ebbed out of his body.

"Pedro," cried Eddie. "I'm so sorry. I'm so sorry. It was all my fault. Please don't die."

As Eddie leaned over his dying friend, the silver card slipped out of his apron pocket onto the palm of Pedro's outstretched hand, the skeletal head with the big eye facing up. The eye bore into Eddie and a smile animated the skeleton's formerly rigid jaw as Eddie switched positions with Pedro and drew his last breath.

About the author

Seth Pilevsky's work has appeared in *What Doesn't Kill You*, a YA anthology published by Indomita Press, Maelstrom, *The Inner Circle Writers' Group Literary Anthology 2019*, *Identity Anthology* by ArrowHeart Publishing, *Tales of the Strange Anthology* by The Writer's Workout, *Stinkwaves Magazine*, *Long Island Literary Journal*, *Literally Stories*, *50-Word Stories* and *Memoir Magazine*. Some of his flash fiction pieces have been translated into Arabic and published in the Saudi Arabian anthology, الرجل الذي يحب العناق (*The Man Who Loves to Hug*). He maintains a blog at spilevsky.com.

Time to Say Goodbye

Karítas Hrundar Pálsdóttir

Peddles going around and around. Onward. A flock of cyclists moving in unison, alongside the motor traffic. Hands used as signals – left, right, stop. A group forms of people who don't follow the blue strip of paint across the intersection but instead wait in a corner until the lights change and they can make their left turn. The path leads them onto Lille Langebro, a cycle bridge, where walking is not permitted, and there – steadfastly moving at twenty kilometres per hour – is our protagonist.

It's me, Adomas.

I'm on my way to work, just like all the other cyclists who occupy the streets of Copenhagen in the early morning. It's a Friday in week nine. (It's a curious Danish quirk to plan everything by the week; just means it's early March). My mind is occupied by the argument I had with Ernesta last night. Like most of our quarrels, it was about our son. He's just started grade 0, which makes him five, no, six. Mykolas knows that we're moving back to Vilnius one day, and I've told him about the teaching position I've got lined up, but he's too young to have any real sense of time. Three years may as well be ten. For him, Christmas was ages ago. I don't see why we should talk to Mykolas about our upcoming move until we bring out the suitcases and start packing things away, say two weeks prior to departure. He should be free to play with his pirate ship and not worry about the future. That's my opinion, but Ernesta wants to tell him now. She says three months will pass by quickly, but to Mykolas it's still winter. Yes, spring is within reach, but summer– that's something else altogether. That's why we're taking the matter to court, so to speak, settling on obtaining a third party's opinion. I promised to ask Signe what she thinks today.

I put out my right hand and make a turn, press the brakes slowly until the bicycle comes to a halt and swing one foot over the saddle until it touches the ground. I walk. I lock up my bike and go to my office shared with Andreas and Kirsten, the two other postdocs. I intend to read and update my bibliography, but like so often my time gets sucked up by never-ending emails and it's time for Friday's *morgenbrød*, networking of the best kind.

"*God morgen,*" I say to Signe, who's pouring coffee into her Signe mug.

My Adomas mug is not on the dish rack where I left it before leaving yesterday. I check the cabinet to see if anyone has put it away. The shelves are full of identical mugs with the University logo on one side and staff members' names on the other side, but my name is not among them. I rub my throat before opening another cabinet and taking out one of the unlabelled mugs that are meant for guests. I fill the cup. My eyes are transfixed by the blank space. It's like my name has been wiped away, like I was never here.

Everyone has arrived now. It's fairly informal, with us sitting and standing as we please, but no one dares disobey the unwritten rules of *hvad er det denne gang?* – first you eat a bread roll and then you move on to the *winerbrød*. (It's funny how in Denmark, Danish pastries are affiliated with Vienna.) Savoury before sweet, logic that would make my mum happy. The plate with the *winerbrød* gets passed to me and I take one before passing the plate on to Signe, who happens to be standing next to me. There's no postponing it now; the weather has been discussed and the commute to work, the noise from the construction site that can be heard through the closed windows, and who's coming to next week's retirement party.

"*Undskyld, Signe,*" I say. "*Jeg har noget jeg gerne vil spørge dig om.*"

"*Ja?*"

She's all ears. From the sparkle in her eyes, I can see the topic is one she's passionate about, but I probably shouldn't be surprised given she was a diplomat for many years before turning to academia. As I listen to her reply, I find myself fixated on her pronunciation, the potato-in-the-mouth kind of creaky voice. I've yet to master the *stød*. Bottom line is, I've lost the argument. Signe stands with Ernesta on this one. There's no time to lose; she would have started introducing the idea of moving as early as Christmas if she were in our shoes.

I nod my head, taking this all in.

She recommends I read this American book that's all about children growing up away from their passport country and has a chapter on transitions and goodbyes.

"*Jeg kan faktisk låne dig min kopi, ja, jeg kommer lige tilbage.*"

And she's gone and I can't help to think how typical this is. I just wanted her opinion and now she's given me homework. I guess scholars, whatever their specialisation, just can't help but cite sources and give out reading recommendations.

"*Hvordan går det?*" Andreas has made his way to me.

I blink fast, and way too frequently, but after a few seconds of silence, I utter a polite reply. Why did he have to come over? We see each other every day in the office we share. Now is our opportunity to mingle with our other colleagues, but no, I'm stuck talking to Andreas. I've nothing against Andreas. He's a methodology genius. He just can't take a hint. And I can't say no. So somehow, we're co-authoring an article for submission in a peer-reviewed journal, and I have to deal with his perfectionism and obsession over silly things like the new APA guidelines. Andreas is telling me all about his plans for the weekend when Signe comes back. She waits for a pause in our conversation before handing her book over to me. Andreas uses the opportunity to take a sip of his coffee, and I notice his mug doesn't say Andreas but Adomas. Of course, he's the one who took it.

"*Bare husk at aflevere bogen før I går,*" Signe says.

I take a deep breath and thank her. There's no use being cross with Andreas; I'm leaving in three months. I'll have to remember to return the book.

As I walk down the hallway back to the office, I call Ernesta and tell her she's won.

Hands meeting in a tight grip, and shaking in the air, once, twice, before breaking apart. Mouths opening to utter greetings. And closing again. Ears turning to catch replies. Lips stretching to form smiles. The guests automatically form a line, not unlike the Danish flag bunting hanging across the ceiling. Each link in the chain connected to the birthday girl. Newcomers congratulate her and then make their way along the semi-circle, shaking hands with – relatives, friends, colleagues, acquaintances, strangers – everyone who has arrived before them.

Me included.

I'm the guy without a tie standing next to Ernesta and Mykolas towards the beginning of the line with the other early birds. It's a Sunday and I couldn't care less what week it is. I just know it's April and we're celebrating Kirsten's fortieth. (No grey hairs so far, but there's no denying I'll soon be middle-aged myself.) We're here to have a good time, but seeing Kirsten, seeing Andreas, greeting all these different colleagues who also got invited, it's difficult to separate play from work. I'm trying not to think about yesterday's interviews, but the more I try not to think about them, the more vivid they become in my mind. Me listening to applicants who are hoping to be selected, hoping to fill the new three-year position, the empty desk in the postdoc office. My desk. They're looking for someone to warm my chair while I'm still sitting in it.

"*Goddag!*"

I don't recognise the eager woman, but Ernesta reminds me she's Cecilia's mom and then I notice the girl from Mykolas' class whose hair is always in two pigtails. How do they know Kirsten?

"*Danmark er et lille land,*" Cecilia's mom says. "*Jeg er Kirsten's kusine.*"

Of course, they're cousins.

Mykolas and Cecilia insist we sit at the same table, so we do. First on the program is *frokost* and they're serving open-faced sandwiches. I pick a roast beef *smørrebrød* for myself and help Mykolas put one with eggs on his plate. I don't get what's festive about eating foods you get every day. Danish people eat everything on rye bread: mackerel in tomato sauce, liver pâte with beetroot, salami with remoulade, potatoes with parsley, even dried figs and chocolate. When Mykolas was in *børnehave,* the kindergarten teachers used to give us daily reports of how many quarters of rye bread he'd eaten. Rye bread is inescapable, like the pigs and the carrots and the windmills and the Legos. We'll be here all day; there are four more meals on the program, but first a game of kickball, and then there'll be speeches and *fællesange.* I bet the printouts will include a song or two by "good old" Kim Larsen. What's with that guy, anyway? If I hear "Papirklip" one more time, I swear I'll– What? Scream? Puke? Shit myself?

Ernesta and Cecilia's mom talk on and on about their common interest, the kids. Meanwhile the kids are getting restless. I don't blame them. Adults tend to have an awful lot to talk about. I ask Mykolas if he wants the paper and crayons we brought along.

He jumps in his chair. *"Taip! Aš parodysiu Cecilijai, kaip nupiešti piratų laivą!"*

"Gerai sugalvojai," I say.

Cecilia follows our conversation with curiosity and then asks what we said. Mykolas sums it up by saying that his dad "wants" him to show her how to draw a pirate ship. That might be stretching the truth a bit.

Cecilia's dad is in the offshore wind industry, go figure, and he doesn't seem capable of talking about anything else. I'm used to being around nerds who talk on and on about punctuation in early modernist writing or the diet of the great auks before they went extinct, but a monotonal lecture on windmills does not hold my interest. This guy has a sharp nose and round green eyes. He looks nothing like Cecilia. I bet she's not even his biological daughter; whether he knows it or not; his wife must have had an affair– What's wrong with me! Bloody hell. It's not like I'll be stuck talking to the poor bastard for the next twelve hours. The kickball should be starting soon. Still, I excuse myself, saying I must go say hi to a colleague without having any intention of actually doing so, but as I get away from the table, Andreas catches my eye and I feel obliged to walk over to him and his wife. When Andreas asks me if I finished proofreading our article, I regret not acting like I didn't notice him. The deadline is next week, but who wants to talk about work at a party? I don't. Andreas' wife mercifully changes the subject.

"Jeg har endelig set filmen du anbefalt. Den var god!" she says and gives me her analysis.

I have no recollection of recommending this documentary to Andreas' wife, but her critique is a breath of fresh air. The teacher in me would give her a ten for initiative, that's twelve with the Danish inflation. (Don't get me started about Danish numbers: You shouldn't have to do maths every time you want to count in tens from forty to ninety!). Talking about this film makes me think of another film, but I refrain from giving out more homework. I simply tell Andreas' wife I'm glad she liked it.

Marching: Right, left, right, left – putting one foot in front of the other. Walking is a repetition of motion, sound, scenery. Step after step. Creak after creak. Property after property. The people move forward, passing red brick houses and mailboxes in driveways, cars too, and bicycles. Green front lawns are fenced off by flowers, bushes, rails. Leading the way, a yellow Labrador Retriever on a leash. At the other end, four screaming children. Right behind them – walking briskly to keep up – is a group of adults.

I'm one of them, of course. This is my story, there's no getting rid of me.

It's a Saturday in week 21 and Ernesta has really started stressing about the move, so I suggested we send Mykolas by himself to this playdate at Cecilia's house. That way we could start packing or run errands or whatever, but she shot down the idea. Apparently, we need to make as many memories as possible and Mykolas needs our support as he says goodbye to his friends one by one. And for that reason, we're all spending the day in the company of Mykolas' friends Cecilia and Lars and their families. And of course it's a given when Danish people get together for a lazy afternoon with friends that a walk around the neighbourhood is on the agenda.

The kids disappear into a driveway, and I realise we've walked in a circle. We're back where we started. We follow the children into the backyard. They run around in the grass, chasing the poor dog, while we take a seat on the deck. Cecilia's mom brings out drinks. The kids seem content with blackcurrant concentrate. I know it's a treat for Mykolas, who rarely gets sweet *saftevand.* We adults get offered pilsner, and Cecilia's dad takes off the bottle cap and hands me one.

"*Mange tak,* " I say. He's a good host.

The smell of newly mowed grass and taste of Carlsberg feel almost like summer. Drinking it out of the bottle is so much more enjoyable than drinking from a can or a glass. It's easy here, buying beer in abundance. You just borrow the plastic beer crate and then return it when you take the empty bottles to the store for recycling. You can do it all in one trip, recycle it right there in the grocery store and you even get your deposit back. But beer's a lot cheaper in Lithuania.

"*Skål.*" Cecilia's dad raises his bottle.

I smile and clink my bottleneck with his. "*Į sveikatą,*" I say and explain that's how we say it in Lithuanian.

Lars' dad tries to repeat what I said and suggests we drink to our hosts. Cecilia's mom says that the pleasure is all theirs. If Danish people are good at anything (other than playing handball, inventing the dry cell battery, and writing fairy tales – I mean, they've got plenty of achievements), it's *hygge.* They really know how to create a cosy atmosphere and live in the moment, enjoying the company of friends and family. They work hard but play even harder, just like the kids jumping on the trampoline, light and free.

Cecilia's mom asks Ernesta what she'll miss about Denmark. Ernesta doesn't answer exactly, but says that before leaving, she wants to go to Tivoli one last time, and she doesn't know if she'll get around to it, but she'd love to go visit a work colleague in Århus. At least it should be easy to squeeze in a few trips to the hot dog stand on Rådhuspladsen. She and Mykolas share a love for *rød pølse.*

"*Hvad vil du komme til med at savne?*" Cecilia's mom asks me.

I don't answer. Someone screams on the trampoline, and I run over. It's not Mykolas, but Lars' little brother. He doesn't seem hurt, just shocked from whatever fall he took. I suggest they take a break from jumping and running around, do something quiet like drawing. The kids follow me to the deck and Mykolas gets his hands on a few bottle caps.

"*Penger!*" he says.

Cecilia grabs some more and says there's so many, they're rich. I see where this is going: Mykolas has infected his friends with stories of pirates and treasures.

"*Vi glæder os til Sankt Hans Aften,*" Cecilia's mom says.

Midsummer is a lovely time in Denmark. I look forward to it too. Every year, there are bonfires, and though I don't care for the tradition of burning a scarecrow made to look like a witch (some parts of history shouldn't be celebrated), I enjoy weaving dough on a tree branch and baking *snobrød* over the open fire. It goes well with hot dogs and then for dessert, marshmallows. *Skumfiduser*. It's my favourite Danish word; the twists and turns my mouth takes when pronouncing it make me smile. It even sounds gooey.

"*Ska vi har snobrød?*" Lars asks.

His mom explains that there won't be any today, but yes, on St. Hans Day, there'll be plenty.

"*Og hylleblomstsaft?*" he adds.

She laughs and assures him that yes, there'll also be elderflower concentrate.

"*Æ, hvor jeg glæder mig,*" Mykolas chimes in. His excitement makes him stand on his tiptoes.

Ernesta clears her throat and explains to Mykolas that we'll actually be in Lithuania by then.

"*Tada mes būsime namuose su seneliu ir močiute.*"

I hadn't realised, but of course we'll be there. But we get elderflowers in Lithuania. We could even light a fire.

Cecilia's mom comments on how sweet the photo of Lars and his brother on the invitation is, the two of them in front of last year's bonfire. Then she notices Mykolas' rapid blinking and puts two and two together. His eyes fill up with tears.

"*Undskyld, jeg havde ikke tænkt, jeg mener, det er ærgerligt I ikke vil være har,*" she says.

That's right, we won't be here, and it sucks. Lars' mom starts apologising for not sending us an invitation, saying she knew we'd be back in Lithuania by Midsummer.

We know! An invitation would have been nice, nonetheless.

Rolling across the floor, the wheels of the suitcase make a rattling sound. One suitcase. Two. Three. Four. Five. Six large suitcases standing up against the wall by the front door. Lying in front of them are three carry-on bags. They're shut but not zipped up, leaving room for toothbrushes and pyjamas. Balanced on top of one of the suitcases is a thick scholarly book. Something brushes up against it and the book starts to fall – towards the bare wooden floor – but someone catches it last minute.

Yes, I do, who else?

I'm wide awake, can't sleep. June is here. It's week 26, a Wednesday, the night before departure. I flick through Signe's book. We'll have to make a stop at the office on the way to the airport so I can return the book. No, that won't work; I don't have my ID card anymore and the building will be locked in the early hours.

I scan the table of contents and pick the chapter on transitions. There's a section about the importance of reconciliation: "Is there a relationship in your life that is full of tension, but you ignore it because you're leaving?" Andreas. I haven't been honest with him for months. I've not addressed my irritation with him. I've been avoiding conflict. I flick my eyes over the page looking for the experts' solution. "Forgive and be forgiven". Feels a bit too late for that.

Next section talks about affirmation: "Validate your relationships by showing your appreciation for them. Express your gratitude". Thank you, Signe, for lending me this book I didn't want to borrow. I rub my eye, then keep reading.

The chapter moves on to farewells. Turns out Ernesta wasn't too far off. The experts stress the importance of saying goodbye to people, places, pets, and possessions. They even suggest making rituals out of it. Sounds silly, but I think Mykolas would love it. I check the clock on my phone: one hour until the alarm. I find a crumpled to-do-list in my pocket and smooth it out, so the paper can function as a bookmark. I leave Signe's book by the suitcases and walk down the hall, close the door to our bedroom to allow Ernesta to sleep a bit longer, and then go to Mykolas and wake him up.

"*Pabusk, bičiuli.*"

I tell him there's something I'd like to do with him before we go. I pick up his backpack, which I know contains paper and crayons for the flight, and lead him to the kitchen table. I explain the project: we each fill a piece of paper with words and pictures that help us say goodbye, maybe a bit like a thank-you card. Mykolas picks up a red crayon and starts filling his page with hearts. I stare at mine and then start writing a letter to Denmark.

Thank you for the opportunity, the joy, and challenges,
teaching me I don't like Kim Larsen but love Carlsberg,
the Midsummer's bonfire, the Danish pastries, and the

parties that go on for hours… I'm sorry Andreas, I wish I'd been more honest with you. Thank you for the collaboration. We make a good team after all. We get things done—

"*Aš jau,*" Mykolas says.

I look at his paper and it's full of colours. He's drawn our family and friends, including Cecilia – according to the two pigtails – and Danish flags and hot dogs and in the corner is a pirate ship and a casket of golden treasures. The word echoes in my head. Treasure. Treasure. Treasure.

"*Kai ką sugalvojau.*"

My idea is we bury our treasures, plant our goodbyes in the backyard, and Mykolas is all for it. I step outside to retrieve a shoe box Ernesta threw out last night and we fold up our letters and put them in the box. Mykolas points out how it still looks empty and rustles through his backpack. The beer caps chime as they fall onto the cardboard. He's got something else too, he says, and waves a picture in my face. If I'm not mistaken, it's the pirate ship he drew at Kristen's party, but what do I know? He's made numerous identical paintings this year.

"*Ką tu pridėsi?*" he asks me.

What am I going to add? I go to my carry-on bag and feel my way through the folded-up clothes and books until I touch the cold clay. It's my Adomas mug. It'll be out of place in my office in Vilnius. It belongs here. There must be other things I can add. It would be symbolic to burry Signe's book, but it's hers, not mine, and I'd better return it. I'll do it by mail if all else fails. I flick through the book, and it opens to the chapter on farewells. The bookmark-slash-to-do-list is there, and I pull it out and place it in the box before closing it. Mykolas has got his hands on a blank piece of paper; that'll be the treasure map. We put jumpers on over our pyjamas and step out into the brisk morning air.

While I find a shovel in the garden shed and dig a hole by the larch, Mykolas draws a picture of the backyard. I call him over when the hole is deep enough, and we place the box gently in the middle before taking turns covering it up. To even it out, Mykolas jumps a few times on the dirt pile.

"*Farvel. Farvel. Farvel.*" He sings his goodbyes, in Danish.

We look at his map together and with a black crayon, Mykolas makes a large X next to the tree he's drawn.

About the author
Karítas Hrundar Pálsdóttir is the author of two flash fiction collections published by Una útgáfuhús in Iceland, *Árstíðir* (2020) and *Dagatal* (2022), for which she received The Icelandic Language Council Award 2022 and the Icelandic Gender Equality Fund 2020. Karítas became the first Icelander to complete a PhD in creative writing upon passing her viva from the University of East Anglia in 2023. She has lived in Iceland, Denmark, Minnesota, Japan, Spain, and England.

Where the Land Ends

Clare Dean

The woman in the red coat is nearing the end of the world. She gets off the bus in Mousehole, not far from Lands' End. She'd imagined it would be cold, that a frigid December wind coming off the sea would provide a legitimate reason for her shivering. But it's neither cold nor warm, just a middling, indescribable nothingness she can't blame for anything, including her fall. When she trips and stumbles forward, a navy-coated passer-by does not help, though she slows, for a moment, grudgingly assessing whether she'll be required to do something, to assist this stiletto-heeled stranger. But the red-coated woman picks herself up, and scrambles anxiously to examine her phone, the screen of which is uncracked, before inspecting grazed hands. She hears the passerby's thoughts as clearly as her mother's. *Who does she think she is, wearing boots like that in a place like this? Not a Cornwall dresser.* Not a Cornwall anything.

Just calm down. The tension she carries is painful and zigzag energy saws at her nerves. *It's not helpful, getting worked up.* She stops at a café to wash the dirt off her stinging palms in a minute bathroom, where she also rubs away a smear of mascara from under her eye. She orders a coffee she doesn't want and shouldn't have that tips her shivering into shaking. It is too much, being here. She is too worked up to let herself be distracted. Most people would not go Christmas shopping in such a condition. But her generation was hauled up by the "just get on with things" one before her, advised to listen to cheery music even when manically depressed, to "just forget about" sexual assaults, to smile through life's problems, because people go through far worse.

You have your health. Maybe. The quaking continues. She's waiting for bad news. She clenches her teeth and continues onwards, determined to shop in this speck of a Cornish village she rarely visits. Penzance may have been a more reasonable choice of shopping destination, given the mass of shops and deals and lack of cobblestones. But it would have been too frantic, too consuming. She thought she'd be able to disappear in Mousehole, only remembering its charm, its toy village shrunkeness that reminded her of being a child and the keyrings she'd made from crisp packets baked in the oven until they were miniature versions of themselves; or the tiny ceramic nightlight shaped like a cottage she'd had as a child. Little and remote, the village was an incongruous object barnacled onto the coastline. She'd forgotten that visiting Mousehole felt like being trapped inside a diorama, tightly contained within the village's stone angles, clearly visible to the rest of the bay, and then facing that maddening expanse of sea beyond – a reminder of the liberty she does not have, of her smallness. Today the village's "charming" aloof grey stone drags her mood further hell-ward, as does the disappointed dishcloth sea and dirty sky that straddles it.

You love Christmas shopping. She used to, particularly in the villages, exploring the gift shops dressed for the season, stocked, it seemed, for her especially. She was close to alive, then, nearly happy. Today she'd chosen to wear her red coat, attempting to feel festive, a holly berry, but instead feels only conspicuous. Whore-red. Blood-red. Tumour-red. Animal innards clotting on the cobblestones. She senses she's ruining Christmas a little more by being here in this state, as if she hasn't ruined it already.

What a shame you can't be there. She'd conceded that Josh would prefer Christmas with his father and extended family, repeating the same holiday he'd had every year in soulless Basingstoke, the only difference being she wouldn't be there. Absenting herself from unthinking Christmas traditions of Quality Street, shop-bought mince pies and soap specials didn't feel like a hardship. Only her Josh-less-ness did. Christmas was coloured differently without the promise of her child's pink-cheeked delight, of fevered energy. How would he feel now, with her gone?

Well, at least you won't put on weight without all that food. She imagines a wine-filled turkey-less Christmas by herself. A few weeks back, still cock-dazed, she'd imagined it with Roy. Back before she'd suffered one too many insistences that she swallow, before he made her watch Top Gear, and worse, bought those awful brown and white plates from Tesco. She couldn't be with a man with such actively terrible taste, even one she left her husband for. The plates were worse than being made to swallow. At least her husband had *no* taste. He allowed whatever she wanted because his aesthetic sensibilities were non-existent. Neither man had been interested in knowing her, or even understood that there was anything much to know. They slipped through the world indulging in curries and beer, gobbling Netflix. Why wasn't she interested in Love Island and excited to plan beach holidays to Benidorm like their friends' wives? What more could she possibly *want*?

You can decorate exactly as you want now. She hadn't been able to bring herself to buy cheap decorations for her tree erected in the living room window of her sullen flat. Instead, she bought only white lights and made a hundred paper snowflake ornaments late into the night – *were they a fire hazard?* – earning callouses from the scissors she wielded for too many hours. They were disposable. She could replace them with real, shinier decorations in future years when she had more cash. She hadn't reduced herself to inserting new tatty little ornament-shaped symbols of her bad decisions and failures into her life. She thought Josh would be impressed, but he said the tree looked "crap". He went home to the house she'd once shared with his father to enjoy the decorations he'd grown up with – the gold stars, the silver fir cones, the bells, garlands, and little prancing reindeer – that she'd chosen, and his father had been indifferent to.

Come on, just get on with it. The woman in red makes herself enter the first of the four gift shops. Predictably, the village is busy in keeping with the time of year. Double-stacked with retiree tourists making the most of their off-peak discount holidays. The first shop is too small and overly cramped, stuffed with old people in voluminous warm coats, and Christmas versions of every gift item imaginable. The little shop seems wired, over-caffeinated and bedraggled after too much customer pawing, open for longer than its natural energy will allow.

What a waste of money. She can never resist the stuffed toy corner of the shop, having never been allowed more than three stuffed toys as a child. An overly realistic felt seagull has been misplaced in the section. Not meant for children. Most of the toys are too young for Josh – little stuffed jellyfish, rainbows and snowmen, crib toys – miniature toys for little children, not eight-year-olds. Toys they were given when he was a newborn and so all-consuming, she forgot she was a "mother" and gifts like these surprised her. Those soft buttermilk corners of boutiques were suddenly relevant. For her. It has never felt part of who she is, this motherhood. And yet, her son is the most important person, the most important everything. She must give him something special to make him remember that he loves her. He'll want a new game for his Nintendo Switch, or a football, or something else that reflects interests that duplicate his father's. Tasteless, technical boy-smelling things. Anything

209

that connects him more deeply with things that exclude her. Still, she hovers around the stuffed seals, the bears, wishing Josh were six again. She wants to give him something to remind him of her. Just in case the worst happens.

See? You just needed a distraction. She's not shaking anymore, though the exhausted, dead parts of her insides are hoarsely attempting to signal she should be. Her hands are steady enough to pick up the Emma Bridgewater mugs. Rows of mugs decorated with rows of seagulls, rows of robins. Her mother loves them, and she did too, before they were everywhere and lost their charm. Has she already gifted her mother a William Morris print washbag, or just considered buying one before? What would be a more significant gift? Something engraved? Is that tasteless? Would it still seem tacky after her death?

Don't just buy people any old thing. The woman's grandmother had died the week before Christmas a couple of years before Josh was born. She'd already given her granddaughter a wrapped gift. It didn't make sense to imagine it would be significant, given her past gifts, but since her grandmother had died, the woman felt that somehow it must be. It was a set of floral-scented soaps and talcum powder that she knew had been bought from Boots in a three for the price of two deal. She couldn't even use them. She was allergic to anything scented. Her grandmother had known this about her. The woman in the red coat thinks of this last gift as she browses somewhat desperately, uncharacteristically indecisive, unwilling for the final gifts she buys to be pathetic, overpackaged throwaway nothings, and be remembered as thoughtless.

The sun's coming out, a reason to be cheerful! As she walks between shops, the sun spares the woman a tiny glance, weak rays from a momentary gap in asphalt clouds. A singular boat bobs inertly, anchored a little way off the harbour, disgruntled by its isolation.

Little Josh used to love the boats. Maybe once, back when he knew to be happy and carefree, secure in the love of his parents. Before his mother insisted on severing his family, unpicking the stitches of an albeit cookie cutter and bland marriage with an equally vapid affair. She'd rather deftly swapped her child's happiness for a man a fraction more attentive and with a slightly larger cock than her husband's. Apparently, she'd thought it was worth it, traded one indifferent man for a second, one set of beige corners for another. His interest sparked a desperate hope that perhaps he'd really look at her, at least attempt to know her, to understand. She'd thought too much of herself, this wind-buffeted, fickle woman.

It's all your own making. The woman in red now fears that it was her unfathomable longing to be impaled by a man – to be fully and deeply fucked – that brought on her probable illness. That cancer decided to inhabit the space she'd imagined within herself. She'd yearned to be filled with something, and her wish was granted. She'd invited it in. All for a slightly overweight cook in a pub who smelled of cigarettes and fish, whose body didn't quite fit hers, whose hips jutted into her thighs. His textures were all wrong – spongey, fleshy, soft, hairy. He'd told her outright that he wanted to fuck her, and somehow the brazenness of that one thoughtless comment thrown away after one too many gins convinced her, along with Paco Rabanne, that it was enough to undo a life for. He'd touched her too hard or not hard enough, and it was Paco Rabanne, and not he, that forced the orgasm somewhat painfully from her. His was disconcertingly silent. A job done. And now this other alien body – this tumour – had arrived, because of longing for something new. Her punishment for wanting too much, for being a woman in red who wore stiletto boots in cobbled villages. Wanting, not because she thought she deserved more than she had, but because she longed to be deserving.

At least he didn't make a fuss. The ending of her beige marriage wasn't tumultuous, nor full of soap opera tears or recriminations. Her husband hadn't the imagination for it. A little anger fell out of him at first, when she told him about Roy, that she was leaving. "Why did you do it, for God's sake!" It was momentarily exciting, this forced reaction, before she realised the emotion was only annoyance at the inconvenience of it all, of the admin, of "this is going to mess up the mortgage", rather than heartbreak. He hadn't even had the spine to be humiliated. Too soon, she was emptied from his life. Cleared out, like the rubbish he always remembered to take out on a Monday night, leaving her to face a man who smelled of fish and bought ugly plates. The man she divorced went back to the "footie", his Gregg's sausage rolls, Match of the Day, and his pathetic Ambrosia rice pudding with a spoonful of jam indulgences, just like his mum used to make. And because she felt guilty, the woman who wears stilettos in villages let him keep her SMEG toaster and has regretted it ever since.

Still no luck? Never mind. The second gift shop isn't any more inspiring than the first. It's as though each of the businesses in the village have conspired to proffer items for every type of person other than who the red woman needs to buy for. There's nothing for an eight-year-old boy, or a sixty-five-year-old woman who has everything, or a best friend whose only interest is alcohol. Just rows of disappointments. Snowmen candles and headache-inducing scent infusers no-one wants.

Smile at the man. Outside, she recognizes the man from

The Ship Inn as he passes. He's a big person, with long hair and trendy glasses, incongruous with his anorak and ill-fitting trousers. She wonders if his smirk means something – if Roy had told him about her, about the filthy things she'd said to get them in the mood once the initial excitement was overpowered by his smell. Perhaps every dirty thing she said had grown the tumour a fraction larger. The woman in red now worries about how she looks. Puffy? Is the daylight particularly greying after too many office chocolates and too much coffee? Has panic layered an oily sheen over her skin? Or, despite these things, is today a good day? Is she all cheekbones and straight teeth and lit, confident fuckability? Why does it still matter so much, being desirable? Why does she need to be wanted by someone she has no interest in?

Careful! You're always dropping things! The woman's ring tinkles lightly on the cobblestones after falling from her finger. It's colder now and the ring is too big. Reluctantly she bends to retrieve it and push it back on her ring finger. She doesn't like it. It's made of cheap metal that turns her finger green, is clunky and overly celestial with cutouts of moons and stars. It's the kind of ring that a woman who believes in the healing properties of rock might wear.

"Wear this on your ring finger," her colleague – a veteran divorcee – said knowingly when giving it to her. "Then you won't miss your engagement and wedding rings. Help you through the initial stages.' She'd meant kindness. She was a good ten years older than the woman in red and had the colourless look of someone who drinks too much tea, eats too many biscuits, and doesn't get enough sleep. Menopausal, perhaps. The woman in red was unprepared to receive kindness. And the ring, though she detests it, reminds her that sometimes, she is seen. She must remember that untainted kindnesses exist and resist those scratchy bullying thoughts that tend to brutally crosshatch over every good thing that happens. She is not hated by everyone.

There you go, not that bad. The woman has noticed her reflection in a shop window. Mousehole's brave new sunlight is bouncing off her hair, and instinctively, she touches it. It's shiny, smooth, and long, the way Roy liked it. He'd liked to put his hands into it and pull while she sucked on the cock she'd only fractionally preferred to her husband's, that resulted in her living in a flat with no view, with a drastically inferior toaster and only paper snowflake ornaments. It had hurt more than she admitted to herself. A punishment for having hair.

There's more to life than looks. She remembers her vanity and is disgusted by it. Looks are superficial, she reminds herself, though they have won her jobs she was underqualified for, promotions she didn't deserve, and lovers she wanted to win but not keep. It was easy to attract. Easy, even, to make a man fall in love with you. It only takes a few clever comments about books, a few self-deprecating jokes, a held look, and a revealing dress you pretend to have worn by mistake. Be fractionally unusual, unavoidably sensual as you appreciate the obscure whisky you profess to be your favourite. Later, shyly disclose that you don't usually connect with people this way. He'll see you're not mass-manufactured, but hand-crafted. Attractive, but imperfect. It's easy to make a man love you, more difficult to hold his attention. She's ended up with some devastatingly disappointing lovers.

What are you worrying over that for? The woman in red reminds herself that none of this matters. Tumours exist.

The hospital will call any moment now. The woman glances at her phone but there are no missed calls. A youth in a black hoodie skulks towards her and for a moment she finds herself wondering whether he's the angel of death. The world is hanging off its axis and not much would surprise her. He looks up from beneath his hood and scowls. Of course he does. He looks like Josh, that adolescent scowl an expression she may never see on him but that he'll direct at his memory of her. Prickles of undirected panic re-surface. Fear about the youth, about Josh or about death, she doesn't know which. She enters the nearest open door into a gallery she's walked past many times but never been into. Inside, she remembers why, as she faces hunched, depressing little watercolours of harbours under grey skies, and blocky textured paintings with tasteful colours meant to blend seamlessly into bland houses.

Honestly, what awful shoes you're wearing. The room is painfully quiet, and the woman is too aware of the sound her stiletto boots make on the immaculate wood floor. Another place she does not belong. A painting of a flowerpot containing three stems presents itself to her. She thinks that if it were a person, it could "murder a cuppa" and have a "cheeky Chinese" on a Friday night. It is ugly and commercial. Thoughtless. Bland. She hates it but hates herself more for her judgement.

Be polite, say something nice. The gallery owner, who may also be the artist, is watching her for a reaction. She makes herself smile slightly as she looks around, guilty that she's not going to buy anything and wondering if the lack of a sale will impact his own Christmas.

"These are lovely," she gestures. "Not quite what I'm looking for. I need a gift for a very particular person." She smiles and rolls her eyes and the owner smiles knowingly and looks her up and down, forgetting himself, his gaze snagging on her breasts. He's over sixty and she doesn't want his eyes on her. She feels sick, suddenly, her nerves re-frizzing.

You just need a bit of fresh air. She leaves the shop,

thankful for the blast of cold air pushing in from the Atlantic. The sky seems deeper, more dimensional now as half-lit bulbous clouds scatter over the ocean and the sun sets behind the remaining boulder of cumulous grey. A sign of hope, those lit clouds, but surely deep fakery on the sky's part. Seagulls the size of dogs swoop hugely overhead, pretending ebullience, those confidence tricksters. An old woman from The Ship Inn who believes herself clairvoyant passes the woman in red without a glance. She casts no worried looks in her direction. This unsettles the woman in red more. Nothing around her indicates impending doom and it's so overtly non-alarming, that she wonders if it's a trick of the light, smoke and mirrors, if everyone's pretending things are going to be okay, when the opposite is true. She feels as though she's been here before, at the same time and space. Maybe she's in some new fucked-up version of the Truman show. A reality show about people who've messed up their lives. Or are about to be told they have cancer, and that it's terminal.

Well, that was a waste of time. Reluctantly, the woman gives up on shopping and resigns herself to spending the evening online, prepared to spend too much on expedited shipping for video games, and tasteful things from Liberty her mother would never buy for herself. She walks slowly towards the bus stop, feeling the weight of her failures, and of the call that has to come through any minute.

Just pretend you can't hear. As the red-coated woman approaches the stop a lady who looks like her mother is arguing with her husband. They're clutching a huge cuddly penguin each, like the one a five-year-old Josh pled for, and his mother refused when they visited the aquarium. She stops a little way off from them to politely avoid their bickering. The older woman turns, observes.

"Excuse me," she says in kinder tones than she'd

216

spoken to her husband with, stepping towards the woman in red. Not Cornish. "This is going to sound strange, but I wonder if you have children?" She smiles hopefully.

"I do, yes." She prickles slightly with the over-familiarity. It's not a question strangers ask one another. She's also strangely pleased that she looks like she could be a mother. Despite the boots.

"I wonder if you might like this?" The older lady holds her penguin out towards the younger. "To give to one of them? My husband and I had a bit of a miscommunication about which of us was going to buy it for our grandson. We both bought one!" She grins and rolls her eyes. "And now we've no time to return it as we have to get the next bus, and I can't be lugging this thing around me on the train back to Plymouth." Silence. The woman in red doesn't know what to say. "Seriously, if you'd like it, please take it." Another smile.

Honestly, that thing is monstrous! What could it possibly be for? Suddenly, she realises that it's the perfect gift for Josh. Something unexpected, something she'd once said no to, something to live in his new room in her tiny depressing flat, until... Something he could hug when she was gone, that he could remember her by. Remember that she gave him what he asked for. Maybe he'd remember the day in the aquarium, when she'd bought him an ice cream which he ate while watching the penguins being fed the fish. It had been a good day until she'd said no to the toy.

"I... thank you, very much." She reaches out a little hesitantly, embarrassed. "I actually think my son would love it."

"Oh really? Oh, I'm so glad!" The older lady breathes out relief and hands over the penguin. In the younger woman's arms, it seems even bigger than she'd imagined it might.

"Let me give you some money for it." She offers, shifting the penguin under one arm to reach into her bag.

"Oh no!" a hand is held up in protest. "Please no, you're doing me a favour. And I remember how costly Christmas can be when you have little ones."

"Thank you." The woman in red smiles properly for the first time today, as an inch of tension drops from out from underneath her. "That's so kind."

"Of course." A smile returned.

The phone vibrates.

Finally! Now, be brave. It's dark enough now that the Christmas lights that Mousehole is so proud of have finally been turned on. The patient finds them tasteless and disappointing and hates herself for her snobbery. But her eyes attach themselves to their glare as she answers the call.

"Ms. Hempsy?" She recognizes the voice of the oncologist.

"Yes?"

"Dr. Lowell here. We have the results back from your biopsy here and I'm pleased to tell you the growth was benign. There's absolutely nothing to worry about."

"Oh." A breath released. The lights in front of her fizz, blur, fizz again, in conciliatory celebration. "Thank you." The woman's arm feels hot beneath the weight of coat and sweater and penguin. Benign. She hadn't willed cancer into her body. She hadn't removed herself from Josh. It wasn't vanity. Wasn't selfishness. It was… nothing at all. Nothingness.

It's fully dark now. The lights of Mousehole re-twinkle, reflected in the water, jiggling lightly, laughing. *See? There was nothing to worry about!* Maybe the lights are not so tasteless. The woman is headed home to buy gifts that don't carry the weight of her conscience. Normal gifts. Not the last she'll buy after all.

218

The bus is arriving, and she turns towards it, the penguin tucked underneath her arm. The stiletto heel of her boot becomes wedged between the cobblestones, and she twists slightly to recover. Her bag falls down her arm and the jolt forces the penguin from her grip, leaving it bouncing into the road towards the bus. Her son's last soft animal. The one that will remind him of the aquarium. She watches the toy tumble into the road ahead of the bus, before being sucked underneath it. *It must be ruined.* Not wanting to risk missing the bus to retrieve the likely damaged toy, and hoping the couple who gave it to her won't notice, she slips onto the bus where it rattles clumsily out of the tiny Cornish village and further to Lands' End.

About the author
Clare Dean is British, living in Vermont, USA. In addition to writing fiction, she is a portrait artist, publishing and marketing consultant, and entrepreneur. Her first co-authored novel will be published in 2025 with Level 4 Press.

White Elephant

Tom Kirkbright

The phone in the hallway rang intrusively, rattling on the stand and shaking the pen pot.

Clem glanced at the kitchen clock. Just gone 6pm. Nobody usually called at teatime. She lowered the heat on the stove, her mother's words chiming in her mind. *Soup that boils is soup that spoils.*

With a tentative breath, she lifted the receiver and offered a reserved "Hello?"

The voice on the other end was sharp, with a well-spoken, yet infuriatingly false manner. Worst of all it was painfully familiar.

"Ah, Clementine, Constance here."

"Oh, Constance, I'm afraid Lindsay isn't home at the moment; he's still at his Bowls Club."

There was the smallest hint of a scoff. Clem imagined Constance in her leather wingback armchair, twisting her pearls with gnarled arthritic digits and rolling her eyes.

"And what should I want to talk with him for?"

Clem could not muster a response before Constance continued, her over-enunciated words and careful lack of contractions deceiving her true working-class roots.

"No, it is you that I wish to speak to."

This was unheard of. Clem blindly fished her hand in the pocket of her pinny to retrieve the packet of *Pall Mall* and her lighter. "Me? Why, what's the matter?"

"Well, I was due to fly to Salou on Wednesday with Lillian. Just for five nights, but unfortunately, she had a fall this morning, so it's unlikely that she will be fit for travel now."

"Oh no, the poor love," Clem said between puffs of her

cigarette, trying to not sound disingenuous. She had only met the woman a handful of times. "Is she alright?"

"Probably. I mean, it's much too early to say if a new hip will be necessary, but they are keeping her in for the next week to be safe. Of course, this rather leaves me with a sticky wicket. It's simply not safe for a woman of my age to travel alone. Nor practical, as insurers will not cover me if I am alone, you see."

Clem tapped her ash and shook her head at the casual selfishness of her mother-in-law. It certainly explained Lindsay's similar traits.

"It really is the most awful shame," Constance said with a sigh. "I would so hate to have to lose the money paid for the holiday, not to mention that I have already purchased my pesetas as well."

Clem's stomach churned as an uneasy, queasy, feeling washed over her. Like a hare noticing a terrier from across the field.

"Well, I don't know what to say; that really is rotten luck. If only Lindsay wasn't so terrified of flying, he could go with you."

"Glibness, Clementine, is not becoming. You and I both know perfectly well that he would never join me in any case."

Never a truer word, Clem thought. Beyond the bi-monthly duty of taking Constance to church, followed by Sunday lunch, Lindsay was quite content to pay her no mind, let alone attention. In fact, Clem would be perfectly willing to swear that her husband would sooner walk into a towering inferno than board a flight with his own mother.

"No, the reason I called was to tell you that I have spoken with the travel agent, and the good news is that she said we can transfer Lillian's ticket into your name for a nominal fee, no problem at all."

"My name?" Clem asked, stubbing out her cigarette. "As in, me go with you? Me?"

They never did anything together. Constance barely even spoke to her, and when she did it was never to say anything pleasant.

Often, she would just glare at Clem, as if wondering why she hadn't been drowned at birth. And now she wanted them to spend five nights in a foreign country together.

Clem felt a knot in her stomach that tightened at the thought. Had the old girl finally lost her mind?

"Of course, you. Now that the boys have moved out you must be bored senseless and sick of the sight of Lindsay. I should say that you are in dire need of a well-earned break."

Clem hesitated. She could try lying about not having a valid passport. Not that lying came natural to her.

Besides which, she had only renewed it the previous year when Lindsay insisted on a family holiday to France via the ferry.

Though she hid it well, Constance had been quite hurt upon their return, it being the first she had heard of the holiday. The paltry, last-minute gifts of a cheap bottle of red and an Eiffel Tower fridge magnet had been of little consolation.

For a full two months afterward, Constance had refused to talk to Lindsay, so the old boot was bound to remember that Clem had a valid passport. The only weapon she had left in her arsenal was to claim poverty.

"You know, that is such a kind offer and I'd love to join you, of course, but I'm not sure that we could really afford it,"

"Nonsense, dear," Constance interrupted. "The ticket is already paid for, meals are included with the hotel room, and of course I would pay for the ticket transfer. So really all you will need is a little pocket money."

Wait, did she say "room"? Singular?

Clem considered the drastic action of breaking with British reserve. Daring to free the tongue that she had held for twenty years and telling Constance what she thought to the whole idea, but her hesitancy had sealed her fate.

"Good-oh, that settles it," Constance said. "We fly on Wednesday."

The line clicked off and Clem slowly placed the phone back on the cradle, in a state of shock. How did she allow that to happen?

Smelling burning from the kitchen, she returned to her pan of soup to see a surface of bubbles.

Her dinner was completely ruined.

It was ruined and now she had to go on holiday with Constance.

Five days of pure, unbridled Hell.

She covered her face with her hands and collapsed into a deluge of tears, allowing them to flow freely.

About the author

Tom Kirkbright is a fiction writer from Halifax, West Yorkshire. His short stories have been long- and short-listed in several international competitions. His stories usually feature troubled characters in and around the North of England.

As well as contemporary and general fiction, he writes crime fiction under the pen name Billy Brightburn.

He lives with his wife and cats, and is currently working on his debut novel.

Index of Authors

Like to Read More Work Like This?

Then sign up to our mailing list and download our free collection of short stories, *Magnetism*. Sign up now to receive this free e-book and also to find out about all of our new publications and offers.

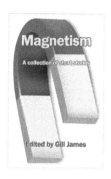

Sign up here:
   http://eepurl.com/gbpdVz

Please Leave a Review

Reviews are so important to writers. Please take the time to review this book. A couple of lines is fine.

Reviews help the book to become more visible to buyers. Retailers will promote books with multiple reviews.

This in turn helps us to sell more books ... And then we can afford to publish more books like this one.

Leaving a review is very easy.

Go to https://amzn.to/3YMIZfZ, scroll down the left-hand side of the Amazon page and click on the "Write a customer review" button.

Other Publications by Bridge House

Gifted

edited by Debz Hobbs-Wyatt and Gill James

What does it mean to be gifted?

Is this to do with a present being wrapped up and handed to another? Does one person sacrifice something to help someone else? Or is to do with having a certain talent? Is that gift always welcome? Does the protagonist make the most of what has been gifted to them? All of those scenarios exist in these stories and there are other interpretations as well of the theme "gifted".

Gifted is Bridge House's 2023 anthology which includes stories by both some of the gifted writers we already know well and by some new faces.

"A great selection of stories by some talented writers"
(*Amazon*)

Order from Amazon:

Paperback: ISBN 978-1-914199-50-9
eBook: ISBN 978-1-914199-51-6

Evergreen

edited by Debz Hobbs-Wyatt and Gill James

Life goes on. There is renewal. Nature endures.

This is a collection of challenging and thought-provoking stories. All stories have an everlasting message and these provide ones that will astound and delight you. We looked for: story, good writing, interpretation of theme and professionalism. All of the stories submitted had those elements. Here we offer a variation to cater to our readers' eclectic tastes. Sit back and surrender to the Bridge House magic.

Evergreen is a themed multi-author collection from Bridge House Publishing.

Order from Amazon:

Paperback: ISBN 978-1-914199-36-3
eBook: ISBN 978-1-914199-37-0

Resolutions

edited by Debz Hobbs-Wyatt and Gill James

Resolve is high. Determination rules OK. Human spirit excels.

This is a collection of challenging and thought-provoking stories. All stories need a resolution and these provide ones that will astound and delight you. We looked for story, good writing, interpretation of theme, and professionalism. All of the stories submitted had those elements. Here we offer a variety to cater to our readers' eclectic tastes. Sit back and surrender to the Bridge House magic.

Resolutions is a themed multi-author collection from Bridge House Publishing

"A delightful and amusing collection of stories from some very talented writers. More power to the short story." (*Amazon*)

Order from Amazon:

Paperback: ISBN 978-1-914199-10-3
eBook: ISBN 978-1-914199-11-0

Milton Keynes UK
Ingram Content Group UK Ltd.
UKHW031344301124
451822UK00009B/295